"She needs to laugh, Ryan."

As if he didn't know that. "But she doesn't need to get hurt."

Two tiny lines appeared between Tina's eyebrows. "I'd never hurt her."

She stared straight into his eyes. Hers were big and blue-gray, with sooty lashes—beyond beautiful. For a moment he lost himself in them. From out of nowhere came the urge to kiss her, so strong it stunned him.

Her pupils enlarged, and he knew she, too, felt something. At the same time, she and Ryan backed away from each other.

"If she gets too attached to you," he said in a gruff voice, "you will."

Dear Reader,

Some time ago, I saw a handsome twenty-something man with a baby carrier strapped to his chest. Cupping the carrier, he walked his infant child around Greenlake, a Seattle-area lake. The expression on his face touched me deeply. I saw love, pride and joy, but underneath, grief and sorrow. In my imagination, this man was a single father who had lost his wife. I have carried this picture in my heart since then, and often wonder about that man and his child.

Ryan and Tina's story was born out of that image. Ryan is a young widower and single father of an adorable little girl named Maggie. He and Tina meet when Tina visits the woman who raised her. Ryan has just moved in across the street. I based Halo Island on two of the San Juan Islands, Lopez and San Juan Island, but mostly the island and the story are figments of my imagination. Yet they're very real to me. I hope they'll become real to you, too.

As always, I welcome your continued e-mails and letters. E-mail me at ann@annroth.net, or write to me at Ann Roth, P.O. Box 25003, Seattle, WA 98165-1903. And please visit my Web site at www.annroth.net, where you'll find my latest writing news and a new, delicious recipe every month.

Until next time,
Happy reading!

Ann Roth

All I Want for Christmas
ANN ROTH

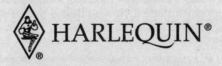

HARLEQUIN®

TORONTO • NEW YORK • LONDON
AMSTERDAM • PARIS • SYDNEY • HAMBURG
STOCKHOLM • ATHENS • TOKYO • MILAN • MADRID
PRAGUE • WARSAW • BUDAPEST • AUCKLAND

ISBN-13: 978-0-373-75192-1
ISBN-10:   0-373-75192-3

ALL I WANT FOR CHRISTMAS

www.eHarlequin.com

Printed in U.S.A.

ABOUT THE AUTHOR

Ann Roth has always been a voracious reader of everything from classics to mysteries to romance. Of all the books she read, love stories have affected her the most and stayed with her the longest. A firm believer in the power of love, Ann enjoys creating emotional stories that illustrate how love can triumph over seemingly insurmountable odds.

Ann lives in the Greater Seattle area with her husband and a really irritating cat, who expects her breakfast no later than 6:00 a.m., seven days a week.

She would love to hear from readers. You can write her c/o P.O. Box 25003, Seattle, WA 98165-1903 or e-mail her at ann@annroth.net.

Books by Ann Roth

HARLEQUIN AMERICAN ROMANCE

1031—THE LAST TIME WE KISSED
1103—THE BABY INHERITANCE
1120—THE MAN SHE'LL MARRY
1159—IT HAPPENED ONE WEDDING
1174—MITCH TAKES A WIFE

To Brian, my husband and real-life hero.
Thanks for putting up with my long days
and sometimes nights in front of the computer.

Chapter One

The ferryboat blasted its horn and slowly motored into the Halo Island harbor. "Music to my ears." Georgia Garwood, known to her friends as G.G., beamed at Tina Morrell. "I can't wait to get home."

It was the first time since her hip replacement surgery nearly two weeks ago that G.G. truly had smiled. And after a ninety-minute drive from Seattle to Anacortes, followed by a forty-five-minute ferry ride, all of it spent sitting inside Tina's car, it was a pleasure to see.

Tina reached across the bucket seats to touch G.G.'s gnarled hand. "You're a real trooper. I only hope that if I ever need hip surgery, I'll be as good a patient."

"You've been wonderful to me." G.G. squeezed Tina's fingers, then gingerly settled back into her seat. "I know the surgeon and physical therapists say I need help for another week, but what do they know? You really don't have to stay with me. If I need anything, I'll just ask one of the neighbors."

Any of the residents on Huckleberry Hill Road, actually a block-long cul-de-sac, would gladly lend a hand, Tina knew. But she refused to relinquish her responsibility. "After all you've done for me, I'm happy to finally have the chance to do something for you."

"I appreciate that, but this job promotion is important." G.G.'s gray eyes grew worried. "You should be in Seattle, fighting for it."

She was right about that. Competition for creative director, a position second only to the CEO of the marketing and advertising firm she worked for, was fierce. Though Tina's only real adversary was Kendra Eubanks, a co-worker who would stop at nothing to get what she wanted. Interviews were to start in two and a half weeks, right after Thanksgiving, and staying on top of things and keeping a vigilant eye on Kendra was crucial. Doing that from the island would be difficult. On the positive side, with the office closed the week of Thanksgiving, Tina was missing only nine work days. Which wasn't so bad, especially with June, her trusted assistant, keeping an eye on things.

"Mr. Sperling always says family comes first, and this is his chance to prove that. Besides, I have to use up what's left of my vacation time before Christmas. It'll all work out," she said, hoping she'd be right. "June and I will touch base every day, and with the Internet and e-mail, I can tele-commute." But vacation or not, with this promotion at stake she wasn't about to leave her work duties to anyone else. "So don't waste your worries on me."

G.G. didn't look convinced, so Tina continued. "You know I haven't been home in early November in years." She usually visited later on in the month, at Thanksgiving, and then came back for Christmas. "Being home now means fresh apple cider from Lindeman's Orchards." She smacked her lips.

"It *is* the tail end of the season, so you're lucky. There'll be a big jug at the potluck tonight, and I..." G.G. broke off, wincing.

Tina bit her lip. "Maybe you should take a pain pill now."

She reached into the backseat and grabbed G.G.'s prescription container and a bottle of water. "Just let me open this."

"No, thank you." G.G. made a dismissive gesture toward the pills. "Those things make me feel as if my head were wrapped in cotton. I don't like that, not one bit. What I need is to lie down. You realize that since I can't climb the stairs, you'll have to make up the daybed in the den."

"That's no problem."

Abruptly, the hum of the ferry's motor cut off.

"All passengers and vehicles may now depart," announced a male voice over the public address system.

Finally. "In ten minutes, you'll be stretched out on the daybed," Tina said.

G.G. gave a terse nod, her pinched face a sure sign of pain.

"How about an aspirin? That might help, and it won't make you feel woozy."

As Tina rooted through her purse, the dozen or so cars and trucks around them roared to life. Because tourist season was over now, the ferry was only half-full, which would cut the exit time. Thank goodness. Tired herself, Tina yawned as she pulled forward.

"You need a nap, too," G.G. said. "Between working twelve hours a day and visiting me at the hospital and rehab center every evening, you're worn out. And way too thin. I just wish I could cook for you."

"I'll be doing the cooking, thank you very much. And *I* wish you'd stop worrying about me."

Following the other vehicles, Tina drove down the ramp, then turned onto the aptly named Treeline Road.

"Look at the trees," G.G. said. "They'd barely started to change color when I left for my surgery. Aren't they lovely?"

The vivid yellow and red leaves *were* beautiful. "They

are," Tina said. No doubt she'd rake G.G.'s backyard at least once or twice before she headed back to Seattle.

"While you're here, you ought to take a walk through the woods. You're too pale, and the fresh air will put the roses back in your cheeks. Help you relax some, too."

"I'll try to do that." Though between telecommuting and cooking, cleaning, driving G.G. to physical therapy and dealing with anything else that came up, Tina doubted she'd have much spare time.

Not that she minded packing every minute with chores. Better that than free time to second-guess herself and wonder if…

No. Lips compressed, she signaled and then turned away from the water toward Huckleberry Hill Road, which was two and a half miles inland and smack-dab in the center of the island.

"By the way, if you need a fax machine while you're here, Ryan Chase—that nice single father I told you about, who moved into Seda Booker's place a few months ago— said you're welcome to borrow his."

Wondering just why G.G. had mentioned her possible need for a fax to the man across the street—was she trying to matchmake?—Tina raised her eyebrows. With the promotion at stake, she couldn't be.

"I know you want me to start dating again," she said. After a bad breakup two years ago, Tina had given up dating to focus on her work. At least, that was the excuse she used. The truth was, she had no interest in getting hurt again. Besides, at her age, thirty-three, most of the men she met were either married, looking for fun on the side, divorced and bitter…or gay. "And I will. But right now I need to focus on getting the promotion."

She glanced at G.G. to make sure she was listening. "As

for Ryan Chase, I wouldn't want to impose on a man I don't even know. If I need a fax machine, I'll drive over to that mailboxes place and use theirs."

"That's expensive, and the store is only open from nine to five. What if you need to send something earlier or later, and what if someone wants to fax you? Using Ryan's machine will cost you nothing except the long-distance phone charges, and you don't have to drive anyplace. So convenient."

G.G. was way too invested in this—she definitely *was* matchmaking. Which made no sense at all, given that Tina's marketing and advertising firm was in Seattle. And G.G. expected her to run the business one day.

"I'll keep that in mind," she murmured, hoping the older woman would drop the matter.

No such luck.

"Maggie Chase is so cute!" G.G. was practically gushing now. "She reminds me of you at that age—full of spit and spunk. A real handful, but lovable all the same."

Tina smirked. Oh, she'd been a handful, all right. Not as bad in G.G.'s kindergarten class as later on. A thirteen-year-old girl, orphaned, scared and alone. But G.G. had taken Tina into her home and raised her as her own, and she and the other neighbors had stuck with Tina through everything. She owed all that she was today to them.

"You were such a good kindergarten teacher," she told G.G.

"Wasn't I? Sometimes I wish I hadn't retired. But at seventy-five, I just don't have the energy to deal with twenty children all at once."

"Maybe not, but you're still a dynamo."

"I was better before this hip trouble. Norma Feather-stone—did I mention she's pregnant at last? Four months along—has been taking care of Maggie after kindergarten since I left town for my surgery. I suppose she'll keep on until this new hip works the way it should."

"You don't need to watch anyone after school. If you'd just let me help with monthly expenses…"

"I don't need help." G.G.'s mouth tightened as she raised her chin. "I manage quite well on social security and my teacher's pension. Besides, I need something to do, and Maggie lights up the house. And her daddy… Well, you'll see for yourself how special he is." She shot Tina a sly look. "He and Maggie are coming to the potluck."

"Of course they are." Tina was sure G.G. saw her roll her eyes at this.

They were almost home now.

"Have I mentioned that he manages the Halo Island Bank?"

"Yes, and you also told me he started a bank in L.A., sold it for tons of money and moved here." Tina wondered just what G.G. had told Ryan Chase about *her*. Well, she'd no doubt find out.

"He's not at all snobby about the money. You'd never know he's wealthy. And he can cook, too. He's bringing his homemade brownies to the potluck tonight."

G.G. shifted carefully, her face etched with discomfort. She needed to rest.

"I know this dinner has been on the calendar for a long time," Tina said. "But couldn't people wait a few weeks? Or maybe you could switch with the Rosses and ask them to host tonight instead?"

The question earned her a dirty look, as if she'd suggested stealing food from the grocery store.

"It's their turn to host the Christmas potluck, and they're so looking forward to that," G.G. said. "I couldn't ask them to switch. Tonight will be fine, especially with you here to help."

Fifty feet ahead, the perky white-and-blue Huckleberry Hill Road sign greeted them. Tina eased off the accelerator, and though there wasn't another car in sight, she signaled.

"Everyone is looking forward to seeing you," G.G. continued. "We're all crossing our fingers that you get the promotion."

"Thanks."

For all their sakes, Tina hoped so, too. Not only had G.G. and most of the neighbors looked after her from the time she'd been orphaned, but they'd pooled their money and paid her college and graduate school tuition—despite the fact that several of them had children of their own. In return, they assumed she would climb the corporate ladder and make them proud. She wasn't about to let them down.

Even if she didn't love her work anymore. She had no idea why or when advertising had ceased to be her life, but the magic was gone. Well, they never would know.

A stress headache threatened. Tina massaged the back of her neck.

"What's the matter, Tina?"

"Nothing at all." She forced a bright smile. "It's been a long day. Are you *sure* you're up to all that socializing tonight?"

"If I'm not, I'll just go to bed and they can party without me." G.G. started to laugh, but broke off, wincing.

THE PEOPLE Tina had grown up with filled the living room and dining room of G.G.'s modest bungalow. Not one of them was a blood relative, but they were family all the same. Tina greeted them with smiles and hugs. After nearly a year away from the island, being surrounded by people who loved her felt remarkably good.

As laughter and conversation buzzed through the room Tina piled food onto G.G.'s plate from the platters that filled the dining room table.

If she craned her neck she could see G.G. seated in the black captain's chair in the corner of the living room. When aspirin and rest hadn't relieved her pain, she'd at last given in and swallowed one of the prescription pills. If she felt cotton-headed she wasn't acting like it. Holding court with half a dozen neighbors, she seemed her usual lively, witty self.

"You've lost weight, Tina," said Sidney Pletcher, a widower who lived down the block. "You're too scrawny."

"Gee, thanks." Tina cast a bemused eye at the portly seventy-eight-year-old man. With his snowy beard, he could've passed for Santa Claus, only he was way too grumpy. Except at Christmas, when he dressed the part and handed out candy. She turned to Rose Thorne, ten years younger than Sidney and another neighbor. "Do you think I'm too thin?"

Chin in hand, Rose, who was trim by nature and a weaver by trade, studied her from top to bottom. "Maybe a little, although when you work hard sometimes you don't have time to eat right. I know that's true of me when I'm working on a project. But scrawny? No."

Tina high-fived her. "Thank you, Rose."

"You could stand to put on a few pounds, too," Sidney told Rose.

Rose pursed her lips and aimed a pointed look at his belly. "Well, you should lose some."

"I'm not fat." Sidney sucked in his gut. "And you're not my doctor."

"Never said I was. But if I were you, I'd get my eyes checked. Because you definitely are overweight."

They bickered like an old married couple, just as they had for years. Yet they'd toured Europe together and spent a great deal of time at each other's houses. What they did there was none of Tina's business. She knew only that they cared about each other. Even if at the moment their matching glares were hot enough to reheat the coffee.

After a moment, Sidney turned to Tina. "It's too bad G.G. can't cook for you while you're here. You'd gain weight in no time. But scrawny or not, I'm real proud of you. My own kids should be so successful. Someday you'll be running that ad company you work for, and I can say I knew you when."

"Won't that be wonderful?" Rose agreed.

Insults forgotten, united by their pride in Tina, they smiled fondly at each other and then at her.

Tina's stomach began to burn, a sure sign that her ulcer was acting up. Or maybe she was just hungry. "You never know, but I promise to do what I can to get there. Anyway, I should finish getting G.G.'s dinner for her."

Both neighbors beamed atta-girl smiles at her, then took their own plates into the living room.

Norma Featherstone, who was a few years older than Tina, gave Tina a knowing smile. "They're certainly intense, aren't they?" She patted her growing belly. "All I hear lately is, 'Eat this... You shouldn't do that.'"

Norma and her husband, Harry, had moved to Huckleberry Hill Road three years ago and immediately had been welcomed into the fold.

"It's all done with love," Tina said as she added a piece of fried chicken to G.G.'s plate.

"I know. Isn't this an amazing street?" Norma looked fondly around the room. "I'm so glad we moved into the neighborhood."

"Me, too." Tina popped a bite-size cheese biscuit into her mouth, then took two for G.G. As she headed toward G.G., the front door opened.

"Ryan and Maggie are here," Susan Ross said from the crowded sofa.

A little imp of a girl skipped inside, copper-colored pigtails bouncing. Behind her, a big man entered the room. Tall, his hair curly and almost too long, wearing jeans and a chambray shirt, he didn't look like a man who'd made a fortune from the bank he'd founded, let alone the person who was the manager of the Halo Island Bank. He hung their coats in the closet, as if he'd been here a thousand times and belonged.

G.G. had sung Ryan's praises, but she'd forgotten to mention his rugged good looks. A woman couldn't help but admire him, Tina thought.

People called out hellos. Maggie waved and Ryan greeted them all with a nod and a grin. Of all things, the man had a dimple in one cheek, which deepened as he followed his daughter to G.G.'s chair.

"Welcome home, G.G." He kissed her on the cheek. "We sure missed you."

"Aren't you two a sight for sore eyes," G.G. replied. "It's wonderful to be home."

Tina handed G.G. her dinner and stepped back, out of sight. Or tried to. G.G. snagged her wrist, keeping her at her side.

"This is my Tina. Tina Morrell, meet Ryan Chase."

The noise abruptly stopped. Aware that every person in the house was watching her, Tina formed her lips into a smile. "Hello, Ryan."

He towered over her, his gaze swiftly darting from her face to her body and back. Tina thought he might be interested. The instant the thought formed, however, a flicker of something—wariness?—darkened his eyes and his expression became guarded.

Completely somber now, he handed a foil-covered pan to his daughter. "Hello," he said, engulfing Tina's hand in his huge grip. "Pleasure."

She barely registered his firm, warm grasp before he let go and nodded at the little girl. "This is my daughter, Maggie. Say hello to Miss Morrell."

An adorable freckled face peered up at her. No wariness there. "'Lo, Miss Morrell."

This time, Tina's smile bloomed naturally. "Please, call me Tina."

"Is that okay, Daddy?"

"If that's what the lady wants."

"I do," Tina said.

A dimple just like her father's flashed on her cheek. "You've got cool hair."

Self-conscious, Tina touched her spiky hairdo. "Thanks. I like your pigtails, too, and those sparkly ties."

"Daddy bought 'em for me." Maggie practically danced with excitement. "Guess what? Halloween was last week! I was gonna be a princess, but then I decided to be the number five 'cause that's how old I am!"

Tina laughed. "That sounds very…original."

"That's what Daddy says, too. Guess what else? A long time ago, G.G. used to teach kindergarten."

"I know. I was one of her students. That's how we met."

"You did? Did you hear that, Daddy?"

"Yep."

For some reason Tina's cheeks felt hot—maybe because

Ryan was staring at her. She kept her gaze on Maggie. "I'll bet you're hungry."

"Uh-huh. Daddy is, too."

A big man like Ryan probably ate tons.

"There's plenty of food left," Tina said.

Duh. Anyone with eyes could see the platters on the dining room table.

Ryan pulled his daughter's pigtail. "Come on, Sunshine, let's eat."

Though Tina was famished, she decided to wait until father and daughter had served themselves. Ryan made her nervous, but she couldn't have said why.

SURROUNDED BY talk and laughter, Ryan kept an eye on his daughter as he filled his plate a second time. Sprawled on an ottoman squeezed between G.G.'s chair and the chair Tina had brought out from the kitchen, she stared at Tina with a rapt expression. No different from anyone else in the room.

She *was* easy on the eyes, Ryan thought. G.G. had pictures of her on the mantel, so he'd known what she looked like. Short, spiky blond hair and big, blue eyes. But he hadn't expected her to be so friendly. The warmth in her expression had surprised him and piqued his interest. But Ryan didn't want to be interested.

Suddenly, Maggie jumped up. Glass in hand, she darted toward her father, deftly slipping between the adults who filled up every available space.

She lifted her empty glass. "Can I have more apple cider, Daddy?"

"Sure thing."

From the jug on the table, he poured a few inches of the amber liquid into his daughter's glass. Maggie gulped it down, then licked her lips.

"Did you get enough to eat?" Ryan asked.

"Uh-huh. Tina's awesome."

Since starting kindergarten in September, his daughter had picked up the word and tended to use it constantly. She was growing up mighty fast—too fast for Ryan. "Awesome, huh?"

He glanced at Tina, who was deep in conversation with Norma Featherstone. He'd heard Tina's story. How she'd made good despite tragic circumstances. According to the neighbors, her mother had died during childbirth and her father had raised her alone.

Just as Ryan was raising Maggie.

Then Tina's father had been killed in a truck accident. Rather than let her go into foster care, G.G. had taken her in and the whole neighborhood had helped to raise her. A beautiful story.

Tina threw back her head and laughed, exposing her slender neck. She was a beautiful woman. Even if she was a little on the thin side, and had circles under her eyes. Most of the type A women he'd known, and he'd known more than his share, were too busy to eat right or sleep enough. It looked as if Tina was no different.

Ryan wasn't dating and he didn't plan to until Maggie was grown up, but if he were, he wouldn't date Tina. No matter how attractive she was. He'd heard that she was hell-bent on someday running the agency where she worked. He wished her well, but he'd had his fill of women who put their careers before everything else.

He only hoped Maggie didn't become too attached to her.

"She's only here a few weeks, Sunshine," he cautioned.

"I know that."

Suddenly her face was serious—way too serious for a

five-year-old. She'd already lost so many of the females she loved.

Ryan's protective instincts surfaced. He would not allow his daughter to be hurt and disappointed ever again. He tweaked her nose. "Ready for a brownie?"

The question did the trick. Brightening, Maggie nodded. "Tina can still be my friend, right?"

"While she's here, she can."

"Can I take her and G.G. some brownies?"

Ryan placed three large fudgy squares on a plate. Walking as if she were carrying eggs, Maggie carefully made her way across the living room. Tina and G.G. graciously smiled and accepted their dessert, and his little daughter rewarded them with a grin that lit the entire room.

While Ryan ate, his gaze wandered again to Tina. Despite the deaths of both her parents, she'd turned out well enough—thanks to the stability, love and concern of the people on Huckleberry Hill Road.

He wanted the same things for Maggie—stability and love. Which was why he'd relocated to tiny Halo Island from bustling L.A. When he'd bought the old Booker house, mostly for the wide front porch and big backyard, he'd lucked out. His neighbors were as warm and friendly as family, and he thought there was no other neighborhood quite like this one anywhere.

Her mouth full of brownie, Tina glanced straight at him. Her eyes widened a fraction, and he knew she'd caught him staring. He offered a stiff nod, grabbed Maggie's empty glass, and headed for the kitchen to load their dishes into the dishwasher.

Jefferson Jeffries, a grizzled man who smelled of diesel oil, followed him out with his own empty plate.

"Tina's a looker, ain't she? Always has been."

Not about to deny it, Ryan grunted as he made room in the crowded appliance. Jefferson didn't live in the neighborhood, but he'd once worked with Tina's father and had been his closest friend. He showed up at every potluck dinner. Nice guy. Nice neighborhood traditions. Exactly what Maggie needed and deserved.

"And she's available." Jefferson winked.

The only flaw so far was that people kept trying to fix him up. Ryan rolled his eyes. "No thanks. I'm not in the market."

People wondered why—he saw it in their faces. In Jefferson's. "Maggie needs me, and all my attention goes to her," he said, repeating the words for the umpteenth time.

If he needed physical relief, he would find it with women who wanted the same thing and nothing more. Though it had been a while, since before he'd moved here.

"I understand." Jefferson added his china and cutlery to the dishwasher. "Tina's dad was the same way. Well, I'd best be leaving. Got to get up early for work. You coming to Thanksgiving dinner?"

Maggie's grandparents were gone, and Ryan's only living relative was a cousin who lived in China and rarely came back to the U.S. He nodded. "We'll be here."

"Good. It's only two weeks away. See you then." Jefferson exited the kitchen.

Twenty minutes later, everyone had left except for Ryan and Maggie. His daughter had yawned several times, but she insisted on helping Tina tidy up the kitchen. Ryan wiped the dining room table with a damp rag. He chatted some with G.G., but her mouth was pulled tight and she looked extremely tired. So he wandered into the kitchen to get Maggie and take her home.

Tina had started the dishwasher. Maggie stood beside her, hands on her hips and head angled a fraction—just like Tina.

Already she was attaching herself to the woman. Ryan frowned. "We should go, Sunshine."

"Do we have to, Daddy?"

"It's a school night. And Tina and G.G. are tired."

"He's right about that." Tina headed for the living room with Maggie beside her.

Ryan followed. He homed in on Tina's backside, which was showcased by a snug sweater and designer jeans. Though she wasn't more than five feet six, she had long legs, a small waist and a sweet behind. Which suited him perfectly. His body stirred, and he jerked up his gaze—just in time.

Tina turned toward him. "It's been a rough day. Especially for G.G."

"I'm all right," the older woman said somewhat faintly.

Ryan glanced at Tina, who looked as worried as he felt. She caught her lower lip between her teeth, then released it, and he couldn't help but notice that the bottom lip was plump and pink, even without lipstick. The upper lip dipped in what people called a cupid's bow. A seductive mouth like that was made for kissing and other things....

Tina blushed and looked away.

Clearing his throat, Ryan jutted his chin toward the door. "Let's get out of here, Maggie."

The gruffness in his voice surprised his daughter, and earned wide-eyed looks from Tina and G.G.

"Uh, please," he added, gentling his tone.

"With brown sugar and raisins on it?" Maggie asked, the smile returning to her face.

He winked and pulled her jacket from the closet. "And cinnamon, too."

"Did Tina talk to you about using your fax?" G.G. asked.

"That's okay," Tina said, as she walked them to the door. "I'll use the one at the mailboxes place."

"I haven't faxed anything since I moved here. Why don't I bring the thing over on my way to the bank tomorrow," he offered, slipping into his jacket. "I'll leave it on the front stoop."

"Thanks. I'll return it before I head back to Seattle." She opened the door, ushering in the damp night air, which smelled faintly of the sea.

"'Bye, G.G. I love you."

Maggie dashed toward G.G. and threw her arms around the older woman, who flinched but managed a hug and a warm smile.

"I love you, too, sweetie."

G.G. was the grandmother Maggie had never had. Ryan's chest expanded, and he was doubly grateful he'd moved to Halo Island.

The heartfelt look on Tina's face as she watched the pair touched him. She'd probably heard about Maggie's mother. She glanced at him, and her eyes filled with compassion and understanding.

Only, she didn't really understand. She didn't know that Ryan and Heidi, a high-powered attorney, had been on the verge of divorce when Heidi had suffered a brain aneurysm—a congenital weakness, the doctors had said. Ryan's wife had died at the age of thirty-one, leaving eighteen-month-old Maggie motherless and confused and Ryan grief-stricken.

If that wasn't enough suffering for one little girl, a year ago Ryan's then-fiancée had walked out on them. And less than six months after that, the nanny who'd been around since Maggie's birth had left them to take care of a grandson.

That had been the turning point in Ryan's life, and his reason for selling his bank, packing up and moving here.

He was responsible for his daughter's happiness and he would not fail her again.

Tina's eyes widened, and Ryan realized he was frowning. Turning away, he herded his daughter through the front door.

Chapter Two

Showered and dressed but still not fully awake, Tina yawned and stretched as she entered the cheerful kitchen. It was almost eight-thirty, but the dark morning made it seem earlier. After the rough night she'd had, it certainly *felt* earlier. Oh, for coffee...

She shot a longing glance at the coffeemaker, but her doctor had warned her against drinking it on an empty stomach. She'd better eat, then.

Unfortunately, she wasn't hungry. The worries twisting her insides into knots had ruined her appetite.

G.G. was her main concern. Having done way too much yesterday, the poor woman had passed a restless, pain-filled night, and had kept Tina awake and running down-stairs at least half a dozen times. At last, sometime near morning, G.G. finally had fallen asleep. Tina hadn't heard a peep in hours and she hoped G.G. managed to sleep late.

That way Tina could work, which was another huge worry. Last night her assistant, June, had phoned to say that Kendra had invited their boss, Jim Sperling, and his wife out for drinks and dinner. The little sneak.

"You should have seen her buttering him up," June said. "I about gagged. Mr. Sperling seemed to enjoy it, though.

I don't like this at all, Tina. You need to do something or *she'll* end up with *your* promotion."

Tina had popped two antacids. "I'm not the type to flirt with my boss, but even if I were, I can't exactly invite the man to lunch. Getting there and back would take half the day. What I need is to impress him with my work."

"You already do that," June had replied.

Tina appreciated the praise. "Thank you. But I need more."

They'd talked a good hour, strategizing about Captain's Catch, a restaurant chain that was currently using another ad agency. Drawing them into CE Marketing, Inc. would be a real coup.

With that in mind, June had promised to overnight the restaurant's brochures and menus. Armed with those and any additional information Tina gleaned via the Internet, she would work up something to knock the socks off Peter Woods, CEO of Captain's Catch, and convince him to hire CE Marketing, and her in particular. That ought to tip the creative-director scales in her favor.

By now her brain should have been humming with ideas. Unfortunately, she hadn't come up with a single one.

Maybe you don't really want the promotion, whispered a voice in her head. Tina promptly pushed away the rebellious thought. "Of course I want it," she said to the silent kitchen. The people who loved her expected her to move up, and she would not disappoint them.

As she opened the refrigerator, the wind gusted, loud enough to be heard through the storm windows. Rain spattered against the window. Tina prayed that G.G. would sleep through the noise.

She started the coffeemaker, then dropped a slice of bread into the toaster. The school bus screeched to a stop out front. No doubt to pick up Maggie.

Drawn to catch a glimpse of the young girl—why, she couldn't have said—Tina headed into the living room. Because she didn't want to appear nosy, she peeked cautiously through a chink in the drapes. To her disappointment she didn't see Maggie, who apparently had scrambled up the bus steps with the same enthusiasm she'd displayed the night before.

Ryan was there, though, standing on the sidewalk directly across the street. His unbuttoned coat flapped in the wind. Gripping a large umbrella in one hand, he waved at the departing bus.

Tina admired his broad shoulders and the way the wind whipped his hair across his forehead. A doting father and an attractive man to boot. With an adorable child you couldn't help but like.

No doubt some lucky woman would snap him up and they'd all live happily ever after. The thought sent a pang through her heart, and she returned to the kitchen wondering whether she'd ever have a happily-ever-after for herself. Not that she didn't appreciate G.G. or any of the other people who cared so much for her. But a family of her own—a man to love, and a child or three, would be wonderful.

The intensity of her longing surprised her. At the moment there was no time in her life for love or children or wishful thinking. The toast popped up. Tina spread it with peanut butter and then slathered on honey, a childhood favorite. Her job was to make the people who cared about her proud, by climbing all the way up the corporate ladder until one day she ran the company. She bit into her breakfast, which tasted delicious. She *was* hungry, she realized.

After finishing the hasty meal, she filled a mug. Added a generous glug of milk, although she preferred her coffee black. Another doctor's order. Standing by the coffeepot, she sipped her coffee and mused. After she was at the top, workwise, *then* she could think about love and children....

A sharp knock sounded at the front door, startling her. As tense as she was, she jumped, spilling coffee on the linoleum and barely missing her shirt. *Dammit.*

The knock was repeated. Now G.G. was sure to wake up. Muttering, Tina set the mug on the table and hurried forward.

She opened the door. Ryan stood before her, holding the fax machine under his umbrella.

"Good morning," she said, keeping her voice low.

"Morning. With all this rain, I figured I'd best not leave the fax on the stoop."

"A wise decision. Please come in." Tina stepped back.

Leaving the umbrella outside, Ryan wiped his feet on the mat and entered. She caught a whiff of man and damp, fresh air.

Studying him from across the street, she hadn't noticed the charcoal suit, dress shirt and striped tie. He looked professional, if windblown, and so handsome. If her heart could have heaved a dreamy sigh, it would have.

Ryan cleared his throat. Blushing, she looked up into his eyes.

The corner of his mouth twitched with amusement. "Like what you see?"

"Um, no. I mean, yes. That is, I was just thinking you look nice. Very corporate."

Her bumbling reply wiped the humor from his eyes. "Thanks, but I'm not into 'corporate' anymore."

Before she could ask why, he shifted his attention to the fax. "Where do you want this?"

Since the den was off-limits while G.G. slept there, there was only one option. "Upstairs, in my bedroom."

The moment she uttered the word, she wished she hadn't.

Ryan's dark eyes met hers with the same interest she'd glimpsed last night—before wariness had taken its place.

"Your bedroom, huh?"

Women probably propositioned him all the time. Tina's cheeks grew warm. "Why don't you set it on the stairs, and I'll take it up later. But do it quietly—G.G.'s asleep in the den."

Ryan nodded. His footsteps solid but light, he moved to the stairs. While he was gone Tina grabbed a paper towel, bent down and wiped up the spilled coffee.

When she straightened and turned toward the garbage can, Ryan was studying her bottom with an expression she couldn't quite read.

His gaze jumped to her face. Acutely self-conscious and wishing she'd spent more time on her makeup, she tugged her sweater over her hips. "I spilled my coffee. Would you like a cup?"

Why had she offered? She didn't want him to stay.

"No, thanks."

Tina was both relieved and disappointed. And in big trouble. She barely knew this man, yet here she was, wanting his company. She turned toward the door, but Ryan made no move to leave.

"So G.G.'s still asleep. That's not like her."

"She had a rough night." Tina couldn't stifle her yawn. "We both did."

"Same thing happened at my house." His turn to yawn. "Must be something in the air. I would've let Maggie sleep in, but she woke herself up in time to catch the bus."

"Too many brownies last night?"

Ryan shook his head. "Nightmares. She's had them on and off since after her mother died. For the past year, almost every night. Mean people and monsters out to get her."

"I'm sorry." Tina understood all too well. "When I was her age I did, too. I used to dream that my mother was frantically calling me, but I would lose my way and couldn't reach her."

Even after all these years, talking about the recurring dream completely unnerved Tina. Shivering, she rubbed her arms. "It may not sound like a nightmare to anyone else, but it was frightening."

She had his full attention now. "When did it finally stop?"

"Only a year or so ago," she admitted.

"Great."

The bleak look in his eyes tugged at Tina's heartstrings. "I'm sure Maggie will outgrow her bad dreams much faster than I did. She seems like such a happy little girl."

"She was born with a sunny disposition—when she's awake." Ryan rubbed a hand over his face. "I'm working hard to keep her sunny all the time. Moving here has helped."

"The island is a wonderful place to grow up."

"But not to live on after you're grown?"

"Not for what I want." For what G.G. and the others wanted. "You can't go too far in advertising on Halo Island. It's too isolated and too laid-back."

"Exactly."

Why would a man who had started his own successful bank give that up to move to this sleepy community? Managing the tiny Halo Island Bank seemed like quite a comedown. Tina couldn't help a confused frown. "There's a huge difference between Halo Island and L.A. Don't you miss the hustle and bustle?"

He didn't even pause to think about that, just shook his head. "A neighborhood as tight as this one? You'd never find it in L.A. Maggie's happy here. That's what matters." A fresh gust of wind rattled the picture window. Ryan glanced at his watch. "There's a meeting this morning, and I'd best go. If you need help with the fax machine, let me know."

Tina nodded. "I will, and thanks again."

"Tina!" G.G. called out. "I need help!"

"I'll be right there," Tina answered in a loud voice. "She can't get out of bed by herself," she explained. "Can you let yourself out?"

INSTEAD OF LEAVING, Ryan waited quietly by the front door. Tina was a slight woman, several inches shorter and a good fifty pounds lighter than G.G. He couldn't imagine how she'd manage to get the woman out of bed, and he wasn't about to disappear until he knew everything was okay.

Standing here, when he was supposed to have left, didn't feel right, and he considered heading down the hall and offering help. But that might embarrass G.G. So he stood still and eavesdropped. In the small house, it wasn't that hard.

"How are you feeling this morning?" Tina asked, sounding both caring and cautious.

"I hurt, and I need to use the bathroom."

"Grab hold of my arms and I'll pull you up."

A few grunts and unhappy groans punctuated the silence. In no time, G.G.'s walker was clattering over the hall floor. How Tina had gotten her up and out of bed was beyond Ryan. The bathroom door creaked open, then clicked shut.

"Need any help?" Tina called, apparently standing outside the door.

"I'm not a baby, Tina."

G.G.'s muffled voice sounded cranky, and then some. Ryan had never heard her be anything but warm and loving. He felt for Tina.

Her heavy sigh was hard to miss. "Shall I make you a bowl of oatmeal?"

"I'd rather do it myself."

"When your hip is better, you will."

"Go ahead and make it, then, but don't forget, I like it thick and lumpy."

"All right, I'll be in the kitchen. Yell if you need me."

Ryan slipped out before she saw him.

THANKS TO stopping at G.G.'s, Ryan was late for his own meeting. When he pulled into the parking lot of the Halo Island Bank, all three of his employees' cars were already there.

Swearing—he'd meant to be the first one here—he eased into the manager slot at the side of the building. He'd intended to drop off the fax machine and leave. But Tina understood about Maggie's nightmares, so he'd stayed to talk.

Yeah, that was the reason he'd hung around. His instant attraction to her had nothing to do with it. He laughed at himself. The view of her exceptional behind as she'd bent down to wipe the floor had been bad enough. And that mouth...

Every time she spoke, he'd zeroed in on her lips. From there, it wasn't hard to imagine what she tasted like—or what her body would feel like under him.

Ain't happenin', buddy. He set his jaw and pulled up the brake.

Balancing a box of doughnuts and a cardboard tray of coffee, he punched in the bank's security code, walked through the double glass doors and strode across the shiny tile floor toward the small conference room off the lobby. His employees were seated around the table waiting for him. Serena, a single mom who worked as a full-time teller; Danielle, a part-time teller barely out of high school; and Jason, the twenty-five-year-old assistant manager, loan officer—and teller, when needed. Ryan liked them, and they seemed comfortable around him.

"Sorry I'm late," he said, setting down the treats. "Help yourselves." He went to hang up his coat and grab his notes and the new signs Corporate had sent.

When he returned, they were eating, sipping their coffee and chatting.

"Thanks for the treats," Serena said.

Ryan nodded. "Thanks for coming in early."

"What's that?" Jason nodded at the large, brown-paper-wrapped package Ryan had set in the corner.

"Signs. We'll get to them in a minute." He started the meeting. "As you know the board of directors expects us to open twenty-five percent more new accounts and fifteen percent more loans than last year," he said, looking each of them in the eye.

Which should have been easy, since theirs was the only financial institution on the island. But many of the residents preferred to deal with one of several banks in Anacortes, a forty-five-minute ferry ride away.

"Here it is, the end of the first week of November, and we aren't even close," he said. "To help us reach our goals, Corporate has developed a deposit-and-credit promotion that starts next Tuesday." Since Monday was Veterans Day and a bank holiday. "Those signs—" he paused to nod at the package propped against the wall "—will be hung tomorrow after closing. That way, they'll be up when we open the doors Tuesday. Right now, I want your input. Do you have any other ideas about what we can do to reach our goals?"

Serena glanced at Danielle. They both looked at Jason. Who drew his bushy brows together and then shrugged. All three suddenly found the cherrywood surface of the table fascinating.

"What's on your minds?" Ryan prodded.

Jason shifted in his seat. Cleared his throat and finally looked straight at Ryan. "We don't see why we should do anything when we'll get nothing in return."

Ryan was with them there. The Island Banking Corporation, owner of Halo Island Bank and banks on several of the other islands off the coast of the Pacific Northwest, paid low wages and offered no incentive pay. Their lack of consideration toward employees was so demoralizing that turnover was through the roof. Even the previous manager had quit. Ryan didn't need the money or the headaches, and in the four months since he'd taken this job, he'd thought more than once about resigning. But what would he do with his time?

For a moment, he imagined starting a bank that knew how to take care of employees and customers as competition. Now *that* stirred his interest. And made him think. He hadn't been honest with Tina this morning. He *did* miss the hustle and bustle. Not from living in L.A., but from building and growing his own company.

But starting a new bank meant hard work and long hours. He'd given up ten-hour days in order to spend time with Maggie. She was what really mattered. Bad as this job was, it allowed him to work nine-to-five, with time off for school field trips. No overtime, no bringing work home and no weekends. Exactly right for a single father.

"Mr. Chase…Ryan?" Danielle asked. He'd asked them to call him by his first name and she still hadn't quite adjusted to that. "Jason didn't mean to upset you. But you asked and…"

Ryan realized he'd been silent too long, and looking stern, to boot. He forced a reassuring smile. "I'm not upset, just thinking."

"You're not gonna quit, are you?" Serena asked, looking worried. "Because you're the best manager I've ever worked for.

"Thanks," he said, wondering whether she'd somehow read his mind. "And no, I'm not quitting."

All three employees looked relieved.

"But if we don't get the numbers up, I could be in trouble."

"We don't want you to get fired," Danielle said.

"Maybe we *should* figure out a way to bump up our business." Looking pensive, Jason fiddled with a button on the cuff of his shirtsleeve. "How about a free gift, when they open an account or take out a loan? Would Corporate go for that?"

For the next thirty minutes, they brainstormed. At nine forty-five, fifteen minutes before opening time, they wrapped up with a semblance of enthusiasm.

Ryan hoped it lasted.

DUCKING HER HEAD against the driving rain, Tina dashed into the Mocha Java, a café and bakery owned by Kate Burrows, her best friend since grade school, and her husband, Jack.

Tall and beautiful as ever, Kate was behind the bakery counter adjacent to the door. "You're here," she squealed, hurrying around the counter. Tina had called days ago to let her know she'd be in town. "I'm so glad you found the time to come in this morning!"

Kate's friendly welcome was just what Tina needed. "Me, too."

She wiped her feet on the mat and hung her coat on the crowded coat tree. Then she and Kate shared a warm hug.

"How's G.G. doing?"

"How're you?"

"Gonna be in town long?"

"Heard you're up for a promotion. Good luck." Kate's customers called out to Tina in greeting.

She knew most of them, and responded with smiles. "G.G.'s progressing well enough… I'll be here until the Sunday after Thanksgiving and back for Christmas… About the promotion—keep your fingers crossed."

The aroma of coffee and freshly baked pastry filled the air. Tina's mouth watered. "It always smells so good in here."

"Doesn't it?" Kate headed for the bakery counter and Tina followed. "You just missed Jack. He's taking Sam to the dentist. She has a terrible toothache—I'm worried it's a cavity. And she's not even six years old."

"Poor thing." Kate seemed to have the perfect family— an adoring husband, a daughter and a son. "Tell her I'm sorry."

"Will do." Kate grabbed a pair of mugs. "How about a cup of coffee and a muffin? On the house, of course."

"Better skip the coffee. My ulcer's acting up," Tina murmured, too low for anyone else's ears. No sense churning up the gossip mill.

"Then how about a cup of cocoa, instead?"

"Sounds wonderful, but I can only stay a little while. G.G.'s physical therapy session ends in half an hour. Can you sit with me or are you too busy?"

Kate glanced at her customers, who seemed content. "I don't see why not. If they need me, they'll let me know."

A few minutes later, muffins and mugs in hand, they sat at a table near the large front window.

"Okay, I heard what you told everyone." Forearms on the table, Kate spoke quietly. "Now give me the real scoop. What's happening with the promotion? How is G.G., *really?* And more important, how are you?"

"Tired, and worried about her." Tina filled Kate in on their bad night. "She's moody and demanding—not at all her cheerful self." Chin in hand, she sighed. "I'm sorry to say that I actually looked forward to leaving her at the clinic this morning."

"I feel for you, Tina, but it's probably worse for G.G. Poor woman is in pain. If that's not enough, she's lost her independence. She's not used to relying on anyone, and especially not on the younger woman she raised as her own."

All true, but that didn't make living with her any easier. "I know, and once she's feeling better, I'm sure her mood will improve," Tina said. She paused to nibble on her muffin. "If I can make it that long without blowing up at her."

"You've been carrying the whole burden alone." Kate offered a sympathetic smile. "You know, Jack can run this place by himself for a few hours. Any time you need a break, call me."

"Thanks." To Tina's surprise, tears gathered in her eyes. She hastily blinked them back. "I really *am* tired, I guess." Unwilling to probe exactly why she felt like crying, she changed the subject. "Your turn. Aside from Sam's toothache, how are the kids? How does Cory like third grade?"

"Loves it. Sam's enjoying kindergarten, too. She's all excited about turning six and having a birthday party at school next Friday. I'm bringing cupcakes and punch—Sam's request. The whole class will be hyped up. Poor Mrs. Jenkins," Kate said, her cheerful expression at odds with the words. "Then on Saturday, we're having a family and friends' party at our house. Since you'll be in town, you're invited. G.G.'s welcome, too."

"Thanks. I'll tell her." The party was over a week from now. Surely by then G.G. would be well enough to attend. "Finally, I'm here for one of your kids' birthdays. About time, isn't it?" Tina meant that.

"Such is the life of a local girl who made good. Think you'll get that promotion?"

"I don't know." Tina updated Kate on the latest. "Kendra's working hard to convince Mr. Sperling she's the best choice."

Kate frowned. "I don't like the sound of that. You need to get back there now."

"You know I can't. Besides, with the office closed the entire week of Thanksgiving, I'm really only gone a little over a week."

"A very important week. You could hop a seaplane and fly back for a few hours, just to bug the competition. Flying would cut your commute time to an hour, and I'm sure that while you're gone the neighbors will be happy to stay with G.G. And I could stop by with treats."

Though the idea was tempting, Tina couldn't leave Halo Island just now. G.G. needed her. "It'll be fine. You'd be surprised what I can do from here with e-mail."

"Have you met Ryan Chase and Maggie yet?"

"At the potluck last night. He loaned me his fax machine—dropped it off this morning on his way to work."

No sense mentioning how much she'd enjoyed seeing him or how she'd invited him to share a cup of coffee. Or her disappointment when he'd turned her down.

"How sweet. Isn't he a catch?" Kate fanned herself. "If I weren't married and in love with Jack I'd go after Ryan."

"He *is* attractive," Tina admitted. "And Maggie is adorable."

"Isn't she? She and Sam are in the same class, and they're good friends. She'll be coming to the party. It's so sad about her mother."

"Don't I know it."

"That you do." Kate grew solemn, then beckoned Tina closer. "There's even more sadness. Ryan was engaged before he moved here, but the woman walked out on them. Then the nanny left. Can you imagine? That's why he and Maggie came to Halo Island, to put the bad times behind them and start fresh."

Trust Kate to know everything about everyone. "I hadn't heard that," Tina said.

Ryan must have been hurt terribly. Maggie, too. No wonder she was having nightmares. Tina felt bad for the little girl and her father. She was curious, too. "Do you think Ryan did something to drive them away?"

Kate shook her head. "Just dumb luck. Or should I say misfortune."

"Well, he seems to be doing okay. Maggie appears to be happy, too." Except for the nightmares.

"Maybe, but a little girl needs a mother. As you well know."

Tina did. All her life she'd longed for a mother. "I'm sure Ryan can have his pick of women."

"You know…" Her friend narrowed her eyes a fraction. "You could go out with him while you're here. Just to give yourself a night out."

Tina wouldn't have minded. But Ryan was G.G.'s neighbor, and going out now could be awkward later. Besides, he didn't exactly seem attracted.

She regarded her friend with a frank look. "I don't think he's interested."

Chapter Three

By Saturday, Tina and G.G. had settled into a routine that was dominated by G.G.'s needs and wants. And her pain, which made her angry and short-tempered. Every weekday began the same way—eat breakfast, snap Tina's head off and complain. Dress, snap and complain, multiple times, on the way to physical therapy. Tina used those forty-five minutes to run errands or drop in at the Mocha Java for a friendly ear and a quick dose of Kate's warmth. Then she brought G.G. home to eat lunch, nap, snap and complain, all the way through dinner and up until bedtime.

After a week of it, Tina was exhausted and her patience had worn thin. Between empathizing with G.G., biting her tongue to keep from lashing back and dealing with all the household chores, it was impossible to devote any time to her job except after G.G. went to bed at night. Tina was barely handling her workload long-distance, let alone developing a knock-your-socks-off idea for the Captain's Catch chain.

Now, having finished lunch, G.G. was settled in her captain's chair, which she claimed was the only comfortable seat in the house. "I need a pain pill," she said, her tone thin and sharp.

Though she'd spurned the pills only a few days ago, it felt as if it had been weeks. G.G.'s pain seemed to be worsening, when it should have been diminishing, and since the potluck she'd taken to downing her painkillers regularly.

From the adjacent sofa, Tina checked her watch. "It's not time yet, not for another hour."

She didn't like G.G.'s sallow color or the dullness of her eyes. Side effects of the pills or something else? Concerned, she frowned. "Maybe I should call Dr. Dove." One of the two physicians, both family practitioners, on the island.

"Don't you dare bother him! You know how busy he is on Saturdays. Besides, I don't need a doctor, I need another pain pill."

"All right, I won't call. But you have to wait an hour."

"You are such a taskmaster," G.G. groused. An instant later, however, she attempted a smile. "But that's why you're the success you are today."

The way things were going lately, Tina didn't feel successful. She felt frustrated and worried about her work. She wished she were in Seattle, and at the same time she dreaded going back. If that wasn't confusing enough, she felt guilty either way. She glanced at G.G. "Do you feel like taking a nap?"

"No, I do not."

"Well, you can't just sit here. You need something to distract you from the pain. Would you like to listen to *La Bohème?*" Her all-time favorite opera. "While you listen, you can work on that sweater you're knitting. Won't that be nice?"

For her suggestion, she earned a sour look. "Quit patronizing me. I don't want music, and I don't feel like knitting. If I can't have my pill, I'll have some tea. I'm cold, and the hot liquid will warm me up. But first, please open the drapes so I can look out. I can't stand the gloom."

Fifteen minutes ago, she'd ordered them drawn. Tina suppressed a sigh and opened them. Weak autumn sunlight spilled into the room. The morning had been shrouded in fog, but at some point the sun had burned through. Halo Island had been named for the fog that hovered over the water, resembling a halo before it vanished, and both Tina and G.G. were used to this kind of weather.

"That's much better." G.G. grimaced as she shifted ever so slightly in her chair.

Alarmed all over again, Tina grabbed the two-tone green afghan that lay across the sofa back. "Why don't you put this on your legs?"

"What for? I'm not cold."

"But you said…"

"Stop fussing over me, Tina. Just bring the TV tray over here, and make me some tea."

As Tina filled a mug with water and heated it in the microwave, her thoughts turned to Ryan and Maggie, whom she hadn't seen in days—if you didn't count peering through the crack in the drapes when the school bus stopped twice a day. Staring out the kitchen window into G.G.'s big backyard, Tina wondered how they felt about the damp cold, and why Ryan's fiancée and his nanny had left him and dear, sweet little Maggie.

The trees had shed many of their leaves, and the yard needed raking. If she had time later today, she'd go out there and…

A knock at the door put an end to her musing.

"Answer the door, Tina," G.G. hollered.

I will, if you'll give me half a chance. "That's probably one of the neighbors, stopping by with a casserole or a pie,"

Tina said in her brightest voice as she returned to the living room. Thanks to their generosity, she had yet to cook dinner.

She opened the door to find Maggie on the stoop.

Bundled in a parka, scarf and mittens, the five-year-old grinned up at her. "Hi."

Tina returned the smile. "Well, hello there."

Maggie poked her head through the door. "Hi, G.G. Can I come in?"

G.G. brightened considerably. "Of course. I haven't seen you since the potluck, and I'm so glad you're here. Why don't you give your coat and mittens to Tina and she'll hang them up? Then drag the ottoman over and tell me what you've been doing. Tina, will you make cocoa and pull those snickerdoodles out of the cupboard? And bring me my tea."

Heartened by G.G.'s more positive tone, Tina bustled into the kitchen. When she returned with the treats, Maggie was chattering away, her words lighting a smile on G.G.'s face. Tina set the tea and two cookies on the TV tray. She set Maggie's cocoa and a whole plate of cookies on the ottoman.

Kneeling, the little girl took a generous sip of cocoa. Wearing a chocolate moustache, she bit into a cookie and made a sound of sheer pleasure. Then she swiveled her head toward Tina.

"Want a cookie?"

"I do, thank you."

"Only one week 'til Sam's birthday party!"

Tina had never seen anyone bounce on her knees, but Maggie seemed quite good at it. While they ate, the small girl issued a steady stream of conversation, pausing only to swallow or sip her cocoa.

"Have you bought Sam's gift?" G.G. asked.

"Daddy says we'll get it on Monday, 'cause it's Veterans Day and I don't have school. His bank is closed, too."

"That sounds fun," G.G. said. "Tina and I are also invited to the party."

"You are?" Maggie threw out her arms, as if to hug the entire room. "Goody!"

Tina laughed. "Someone in this room likes birthday parties."

"Me! Me!" Midbounce, Maggie angled her head in Tina's direction. "Why don't you live with G.G. forever?"

"Because I have my own apartment and a job in Seattle. After Thanksgiving, I'll be going back."

"Oh." Maggie went silent, but only for a moment. "We cleaned the house today. I got to sweep the kitchen floor and empty my wastebasket. And separate the dark clothes from the light in the laundry. Sometimes our laundry stinks." She held her nose. "Then we cleaned Eggwhite's cage. That's our hamster, and I love her soooo much. Do you want to come over and play with her on Monday, Tina?"

For some reason seeing the inside of the house where Ryan and Maggie lived interested Tina. Telling herself she just wanted to find out whether they'd painted over Mrs. Booker's dingy pink walls, she nodded. "If your daddy doesn't mind, that'd be fun."

"I don't think he will. He's drivin' me bats," she said, sounding so adult that Tina smiled and G.G. chuckled— only to end up wincing with pain a moment later.

"Is that right?" G.G. said. "How so?"

"After we cleaned, I was tired. But Daddy wanted to play. We played with my dollhouse. Then we did puzzles. We played catch with my Nerf ball. Then Daddy read from my Amelia Bedelia chapter book."

"All that? My goodness." G.G. shook her head. "That sounds wonderful."

Instead of agreeing, Maggie heaved a sigh, leaned her elbow on the ottoman and rested her cheek on her fist. "Daddy *always* wants to play with me. He doesn't have anybody else to play with."

She looked so forlorn—and so adorable. Tina bit back a smile. "I think maybe you should be grateful. My father worked long hours. We didn't get much time together."

"My daddy used to work all the time. But then we moved here, and now he doesn't." She sat down on the rug, crossing her legs Indian style. "Sometimes I want to play with Sam and Gina, but I'm scared that if I do, he'll be sad."

Tina understood, because she had felt just as responsible for her own father's happiness. Apparently Maggie was headed down the same road. Tina felt for the little girl.

G.G. murmured her understanding. "I'm sure he doesn't know how you feel, honey. You should talk to him."

"No." Maggie shook her head. "My daddy needs me."

G.G.'s expression was weighted with concern. "You're a very special little girl, and he's so lucky to have you."

True, but Tina was sure he'd be upset if he knew Maggie was staying away from her friends so that her daddy wouldn't be lonely. Someone ought to tell him. She made up her mind to do that herself—today. The thought of seeing Ryan made her happier than it should have.

"Does he know you're here?" she asked.

Looking guilty, Maggie shook her head. "He said I could play outside."

"Better call him, so he doesn't worry." G.G. nodded at the phone on the end table.

"Do you know your phone number?" Tina asked.

The little girl scrambled up and shot her an incredulous

look. "Of course I do." She moved to the phone, dialed and then listened. "Hi, Daddy. I'm at G.G.'s."

"Ask him if he wants to come for dinner," G.G. said.

What? Wondering what she was up to, Tina eyed her. Suddenly busy with her tea bag, G.G. refused to look up.

Actually, dinner wasn't a bad idea. It would give Tina the chance to tell Ryan what Maggie had said—provided they could talk out of his daughter's earshot. And maybe she'd also gain some insight into why he was alone.

She wouldn't think about her attraction to him or anything else.

"Please?" Maggie pleaded into the receiver. With a stricken look she hung her head. "Daddy says it's too much trouble. He says no, thank you."

"Give me that phone." G.G. held out her hand. "It's no extra work at all," she told Ryan. "We have a lovely chicken casserole, courtesy of Linda Sewell, so there isn't much to do. Tina doesn't mind making a bigger salad or setting the table for two more people, do you, dear?"

Tina shook her head.

"She says it's fine," G.G. said. "Why don't you come at six-thirty. Yes, we'd love another pan of those brownies. Yes, I'll tell her."

When she hung up, her face was pale and pinched. "Your dad says to come home soon for a nap."

"But I'm not tired. Can I stay a teensy while longer? Pretty please, with raisins and brown sugar?"

Torn between concern for G.G. and wanting to spend a little more time with Maggie, Tina fiddled with the spikes in her hair. "G.G.'s tired, Maggie. Maybe you should go home now."

"Don't worry about me. I'll be fine after I take my pain pill and lie down. Just help me to the bathroom first."

"While you rest, I'll rake the backyard," Tina said.

"Can I help?"

Maggie's round eyes and eager expression were hard to resist. Tina nodded. "For a little while. Why not?"

THE RAKE HANDLE was nearly a foot taller than Maggie, yet she managed to gather a small load of leaves. As she carried them to the pile Tina had started to make, they fluttered away until only a few that had caught on the rake tines remained. Maggie didn't seem to notice. She shook the rake clean, then glanced anxiously at Tina.

The afternoon temperature had climbed to a balmy fifty, and the sun and fresh air felt good. Tina smiled. "You did great."

Maggie beamed. "Daddy says I'm the best helper ever."

"I have to agree." One of Maggie's pigtails was coming down, and strands of hair kept getting in her eyes. Tina beckoned her close. "Let me fix your hair."

The little girl trotted over. Holding still, she let Tina finger comb her hair and refasten the pigtail.

"Your hair smells good," Tina said, sniffing. "Is that cherry shampoo?"

"Uh-huh. Can I smell yours?" Tina bent down and Maggie sniffed. "Coconut."

"That's right."

"This is bunches more fun than playing with Daddy."

"How so?"

"'Cause we're both girls."

"That we are."

With her own rake, Tina swept the remaining leaves into the pile. It was time to scoop them into black plastic trash bags, then put the rakes away until the rest of the leaves fell. But not just yet.

A crazy idea grabbed her. "When I was your age one of my favorite fall activities was jumping in leaves just like these," she said. "Have you ever done that?"

"No." Maggie giggled.

"Want to try it with me?"

"Yes!" Clapping her hands she jumped up and down.

"Come on, then." Tina moved back ten feet, Maggie following.

"We're going to run toward the pile. Just before we reach it, we'll jump in." Feeling silly, but ridiculously happy, she took hold of Maggie's hand. The tiny fingers held hers tightly, and a sweet feeling warmed her. "Ready?"

"Set, go!"

Laughing, they ran for the leaf pile. Just before they reached it, Tina let go of her hand. Giggling, the little girl jumped in, Tina right behind her.

They came up sputtering and laughing and covered with leaves.

"That was fun!" Maggie said. "Can we do it again?"

Tina glanced up to find Ryan watching them.

"Maggie helped me rake leaves." She looked at the mess they'd made and laughed. "Looks like I'll be raking them all over again."

His stern expression was not what she expected.

"Time for a rest, Sunshine," he said, all brusque and hard-faced.

Tina frowned. "If I've somehow offended…"

"Later." He jerked his chin toward Maggie. "Let's go home."

"Tonight, then," Tina said.

"We can't make it, after all."

"But you said we could come." The joy drained from Maggie's expression. "I'm sorry, Daddy." Her face crumpled.

Not at all happy at this turn of events, Tina placed her hand on the child's narrow shoulder and stared Ryan in the eyes. "Your daddy's way off base, sweetie. You were a big help to me. You didn't do anything wrong. If anyone's at fault here, it's me for not sending you home."

Ryan actually grimaced. His eyes revealed uncertainty and confusion. "Tina's right. You did fine." He shook his head, as if to clear it. "All right, we'll come to dinner."

Maggie sniffled and nodded.

"Will you wait for me in the front yard?"

"'Kay."

He didn't speak again until his daughter rounded the corner. Then he gestured Tina closer. "We need to talk," he said.

WITH HIS DAUGHTER in the front yard, this wasn't the ideal time to say what needed to be said, but that didn't matter. Ryan's job was to protect Maggie, and he would set Tina straight.

"Why are you so upset?" she asked, her arms hugging her waist.

Fresh air, laughter and irritation with him had put a pink blush on her cheeks. Several leaves clung to her hair and her coat.

Resisting the urge to brush them away, Ryan stuffed his hands into his jacket pockets and tried to explain. "Maggie's been disappointed a lot."

"All we did was rake leaves and have fun. She needs to laugh, Ryan."

As if he didn't know that. "But she doesn't need to get hurt."

Two tiny lines appeared between Tina's eyebrows. "I'd never hurt her."

She stared straight into his eyes. Hers were big and blue-gray, with sooty lashes—beyond beautiful. For a moment, Ryan lost himself in them. From out of nowhere the urge to kiss her took hold of him, so strong it stunned him.

Her pupils enlarged and he knew she, too, felt something. At the same time, they backed away from each other.

"If she gets too attached to you, she will," he said in a gruff voice.

"Will…?" She looked confused, as if she'd forgotten what they were talking about.

"Get hurt."

Tina nodded. "Don't worry. She knows I'm only here through Thanksgiving. We talked about it."

"That doesn't mean she won't be upset when you go." Leaving him to pick up the pieces. No, he would not allow his daughter to suffer.

"But I'll be back at Christmas."

Which was more than he could say for any of the other females in Maggie's life. Ryan let out a cynical laugh. "That's something, I guess."

"May I ask you a question?"

Ryan shrugged. "Shoot."

"I know about your wife. But what happened with your fiancée and the nanny?"

"You heard about that, did you?"

There weren't many secrets in a small town, but Ryan was clueless as to how she'd found out something he rarely mentioned. He didn't want to explain, but she'd asked…

"Christy—my ex-fiancée—decided she'd rather take a job promotion and move to Texas than get married. Mrs. Miumi—that's the nanny—has a daughter with a drug problem. She moved to Virginia to raise her grandson. She'd been with us since Maggie was a few weeks old."

Either Tina looked relieved by this information, or Ryan was blind. *Why* was anybody's guess.

"I'm so sorry." She laid her hand on his forearm.

Even through his denim sleeve he felt her warmth. It burned into him. "I don't want your pity," he said, removing her hand. "I just want to protect my daughter."

"And she wants to protect you."

Uncertain he'd heard right, he squinted. "What's that supposed to mean?"

"Maggie feels responsible for your happiness. At least, that's what she said."

This shocked him. And cut deep. Ryan swore. "What the hell am I supposed to do about that?"

"Well, you…" Tina glanced past him. Her eyes widened. "Hello, Maggie."

How much had she heard? Ryan spun toward her, his gaze combing her face. "What is it, Sunshine?"

"I'm tired of waiting, Daddy."

He saw no sign that she'd heard or understood. Relief poured through him. It was time to take his daughter home. Even if this conversation with Tina wasn't over.

"Why don't we talk more tonight?" she said.

He nodded. "Tonight."

Chapter Four

After a not-so-relaxed dinner, Ryan helped Tina clean up the kitchen. They didn't talk much, which was okay by him and not all that different from their meal.

Tina had tried to keep the conversation going, when she wasn't casting anxious glances at G.G. The older woman looked as if she'd aged a decade, her face gray and taut, and her occasional comments clipped. Good thing his daughter liked to talk, because without her constant chatter things would've been downright uncomfortable.

Ryan had been no help, his mind focused on finishing the afternoon's conversation with Tina. There were other things on his mind, too; things that had nothing to do with talking.

Like it or not—and he did not—he was intensely attracted to Tina Morrell. He sensed that she felt something for him, too, which made his feelings that much more dangerous. But tonight wasn't about him and his inconvenient sexual desire. He was here for two reasons—because Maggie had begged and because he needed Tina's help and advice. Period.

He shook the placemats over the garbage can. Aside from that, he was extremely worried about G.G. "G.G.

seems worse than she did a few days ago," he said under his breath.

"I think so, too."

Tina loaded the cutlery into the dishwasher, then cast an anxious glance over her shoulder, probably checking to make sure Maggie wasn't eavesdropping. But she and G.G. were in the living room, Maggie reading aloud from one of the *I Can Read!* books G.G. had saved from her teaching days.

"The pain isn't going away, but she won't let me contact her surgeon," Tina murmured, her eyes dark and filled with shadows. "Or Dr. Dove, who's treated her for years. He's the one who recommended her surgery. Maybe I'll call him, anyway."

"Can't hurt."

Ryan scooped leftover casserole into a plastic container. He wished he could ease Tina's anxieties, but he'd never been good at comforting others. As he handed her the casserole dish, his gaze dropped to her lips.

For a moment he forgot what they were talking about. The urge to kiss her was just as powerful as it had been this afternoon. Too damn bad. He wiped his hands on his jeans and stepped back.

"Do you think I should call tonight?" Tina asked.

"Uh, sure." Here they were, talking about G.G.'s pain and he was wondering whether Tina tasted as sweet as she looked. *Really nice, Chase.* Best leave now, and talk about Maggie later. But instead he said, "Want me to stick around while you call?"

"Would you?"

Her eyes lit up with gratitude, making him feel like a total dog for wanting her at a time like this. "I'll wash that dish," he said. "You make the call."

"Thanks. After I talk to the doctor, we'll finish our conversation about Maggie."

While he scrubbed off the baked-on food, Tina dried her hands. She stole quietly to the door between the kitchen and dining room and peered out, checking on G.G. and Maggie. Maggie's voice floated toward them. Still reading, then. By the time Tina closed the door, the dish was clean.

Phone in hand, she gestured Ryan to sit down at the table, then she joined him. She'd reached an answering exchange, which connected her to the doctor. Ryan meant to concentrate on her words, but several times his attention strayed to her mouth. He tried not to kick her foot with his, but his legs were long and this was a small table. More than once their knees brushed. They were both wearing jeans and the contact never lasted more than a fraction of a second, yet the whole experience was erotic as hell. Damned if a certain part of him didn't wake right up. As if he were some hormone-crazed kid.

What was his problem?

Frowning, he scooted back, putting some distance between their legs. Tina shot him a surprised look before returning her attention to the phone. Proving that the under-the-table attraction thing was his problem alone. Man, he really needed to get laid.

"Thanks, I'll do that," she said, hanging up. "Dr. Dove says some pain is normal, but G.G. might be trying to do too much. To be on the safe side, we scheduled an appointment for Monday morning. If she spikes a fever, though, I'm to call him back right away."

"You want to take her temperature now?"

Tina shook her head. "I don't think she'll let me—especially while you're here."

"Then we'll leave." He started to stand.

"We should talk about Maggie first, while we can. She's bound to get tired of reading soon."

Good point. Ryan sat down again.

"By the way, she invited me over on Monday, to meet her hamster."

Tina in his house? Ryan wasn't sure about that, but Maggie had already invited her. "We're busy all day," he said. "She goes to bed at eight. Could you come between dinner and then?"

Tina nodded. "I won't stay long."

Time to get to the point. Ryan spoke his thoughts. "What you said this afternoon… It shook me. I'm responsible for Maggie's happiness, and not the other way around. At least that's how it's supposed to be. I wish I knew how she twisted that."

"You'd be surprised at how often kids take on responsibility for things that have nothing to do with them," Tina said, her huge blue eyes fixed on him. "I certainly did. Especially where my daddy was concerned."

Every time Tina shared what had happened to her as a kid and how she'd felt, Ryan counted himself lucky. She'd been where Maggie was, and her insights were invaluable.

Arms on the table, he eyed her. "Did you ever tell your father?"

"I never said a word to anyone. Like Maggie, I simply assumed his happiness was up to me."

In his mind Ryan pictured Tina as a kid, with all that responsibility. A burden no child should be saddled with. For sure, not Maggie. Hadn't she been through enough?

He'd screwed up again. At the painful realization, he groaned in frustration. "What a mess. How do I fix it?"

"It's not so difficult. Be happy, and Maggie will be, too.

Once she sees that you're okay, she'll stop worrying about you and start enjoying her own life."

"I *am* happy," Ryan said, sounding gruff and defensive to his own ears.

"Maybe so," Tina said, but she looked doubtful. "Apparently, though, you haven't convinced Maggie."

Mad at himself, he swore. Tina reached across the table, started to draw back, and then changed her mind. As she had this afternoon, she touched his forearm, her gentle squeeze reassuring. Unlike this afternoon, however, this time he welcomed the contact. And when she drew back, he missed the warmth.

"How do I do that? I'm not a man who laughs much. I never have been."

"Happiness is more than laughter, Ryan. It's waking up with energy and enthusiasm, enjoying time with friends and loving what you do in life. I learned that from living with G.G."

"Yeah?" He eyed Tina. "From what I see, you're not happy, either."

She bristled. "I am so!"

He didn't believe her, and he wanted to find out what had put the shadows in her eyes. More than concern over G.G.'s health, he guessed. But her problems were none of his business. Besides, this conversation was about Maggie.

"What else?" he asked.

She settled again in her seat. "Don't smother Maggie. Let her enjoy some activities without you, like playing with her friends."

That stung. "As if I wouldn't. And I don't smother her."

Though he did spend all his free time with her. That wasn't smothering, was it? Feeling like an inadequate father and unable to sit still, Ryan stood and began to pace the kitchen, which was too small for the long, rapid strides he was inclined to take. But he wasn't about to open the door for more space, because that might draw Maggie's and G.G.'s attention.

"She's too worried about you to make plans with her friends. If you had some of your own, that would help."

"I do." He kept in touch with several buddies in L.A.

Tina scooted her chair closer to the table so that he could bypass her. He brushed past, catching the smell of coconut—a breath of summer in late fall.

"Here on the island?"

"One or two." Though at the moment he was hard-pressed to name them. Busy with Maggie, he hadn't made an effort beyond the neighbors. He reached the stove, pivoted and headed toward the back door.

"Do you ever invite them over or hang out with them? Or maybe go out on a date?"

Was she fishing, to find out if there was a woman in his life? He stopped pacing and leaned a shoulder against the back wall. "After what Maggie's been through, I don't date. My spare time belongs to her."

"Aha."

Ryan ran his hands through his hair. "I moved here so that we could spend more time together. You're telling me that's wrong?"

"Not at all. She's truly lucky to have your undivided attention. Just, maybe you could find a hobby? A way to spend some of your free time apart from her, in an adult activity you enjoy, so she doesn't continually feel obligated to entertain you?"

Between work and taking care of his daughter, there wasn't time for hobbies. Ryan didn't say so, figuring this was more proof that he was smothering his kid. *Well, hell.* He crossed his arms.

"I play golf, but not in this weather." And not since moving here. "In the summer, I like to hike and fish. With Maggie." He glared at Tina, who suddenly irritated him no end. "Are you saying I shouldn't take her with me?"

Her back stiffened and her eyes flashed—he'd irritated her, too. "Of course not. We're trying to think of something you can do with adult friends, something that doesn't involve her."

With her head high and her lips compressed, she was more beautiful than ever. Ryan pushed away from the wall. "There is one adult activity I like a lot that has nothing to do with Maggie."

Hardly aware of what he was doing, he started toward Tina.

"What's that?" Her eyes were wide and wary.

"This."

Taking hold of her upper arms, he pulled her to her feet. And kissed her.

RYAN WAS kissing her! Caught completely off guard, Tina stood still and let him. Her head barely reached his shoulder, but his mouth was hard on her lips and his hands gripped her shoulders. His bright, angry eyes bored into hers.

Provoked and without an ounce of tenderness or passion—this was no way to be kissed. Tina placed her palms against his chest to push him away. He must've misinterpreted, though, for he growled, the sound vibrating through her. Then his arms wrapped tighter around her, his eyes closed and he gentled the kiss.

Warmth filled her. Her own eyelids drifted shut. Instead

of breaking contact, she slid her hands up his solid chest, wrapped her arms around his neck and pulled closer.

The instant she sank against him, the kiss turned hot and demanding, Ryan lifting her so that their heads were nearly level.

She hadn't been kissed in a long while, and never like this. She opened her mouth for his seeking tongue and lost herself in his taste, his smell…his arousal.

The instant she noticed, her feet were on the ground again and Ryan was backing away.

"Don't know why I did that," he said around a ragged breath. "I apologize."

Dazed, nerves taut and humming, Tina wasn't sorry. Not by a long shot. She *was* confused, though. Hadn't Ryan just explained in no uncertain terms that Maggie was the only female in his life, period? That he didn't date?

Unless Tina was mistaken, those kisses said otherwise. "I don't understand," she said.

"Like I told you, with everything that's happened to Maggie I can't afford to get involved."

Apparently, she *was* mistaken. "Don't worry about me. With a career to worry about I'm way too busy for that, too." Her fingers trembled as she fluffed her hair. "It was only a few kisses."

A doozy of a few kisses. She touched her lips, which felt slightly swollen.

Ryan's eyes followed the movement, darkening with heat. "Glad you feel the same way."

She didn't, though, not at all. His kisses had jolted her awake, as if she'd been asleep since her breakup. Her body was hungry, and her heart. But she wouldn't let herself think about her deep longing for a man's love.

"You probably should go home now." Before she made a fool of herself by falling all over him.

She opened the door to the dining room. And heard Maggie, still reading to G.G.

Thank heavens.

"I appreciate the advice about Maggie," Ryan said as they neared the living room. "If you need any help with G.G...."

What she needed were things Ryan didn't want to give and she couldn't afford to want. "I don't, thank you."

As they entered the living room, the older woman shot them a sly look. Did she somehow know what had happened?

"The dishes are done and the kitchen is clean," Tina said, smoothing down her pullover. She turned her attention to Maggie. "You're a good reader, Maggie, but it's getting late and G.G. needs her rest."

G.G. didn't argue. She looked exhausted and alarmingly pale. Tina tried to hide her concern. She wanted Ryan gone.

Once he and Maggie were out the door she'd deal with G.G., including taking her temperature. If it was normal, she'd put her to bed. If not...

Tina didn't want to think about that. She hoped and prayed that after a good night's rest, G.G. would feel better, and that she would, too.

RAIN PUMMELED the roof, the rhythmic noise filling Ryan's bedroom. If he'd been asleep, the sound would've awakened him. But he wasn't. How could he be, after he'd made the worst mistake possible tonight—he'd kissed Tina.

Lucky for him, she'd accepted his apology.

Trouble was, he'd lied. He wasn't sorry at all. She tasted better than he'd ever imagined. She'd kissed him back, too, with plenty of enthusiasm, her soft curves pressing against him. It had been sweet torture, and not nearly enough.

Now he wanted more, a whole lot more. And he figured she did, too.

Muttering, he flipped onto his side. Then onto his back. He couldn't get comfortable—he was too damn mad at himself. What had he been thinking?

He imagined Tina in his bed right now, her thighs gripping his waist and her head thrashing on his pillow. Driving him higher and higher with her frantic need.

A certain part of him throbbed and stood at attention. Ryan groaned. He couldn't go there, not with Tina. Work was the most important thing in her life, and God knew, he'd had more than his fill of career-oriented women. They never stuck around.

Getting tangled up with her would be bad news, with his daughter getting the short end of the deal. Maggie needed stability, and Ryan intended to give her that.

In other words, Tina was out of the picture.

What a relief she was leaving after Thanksgiving. Between now and then, he'd steer clear of her. Except that she was coming over Monday night to meet Maggie's hamster. Ryan swore. After that, then.

And he'd make sure Maggie understood that Tina only visited the island a few times a year.

Maggie. How in hell was he supposed to convince her that his happiness was *his* problem, and not hers?

Clueless and feeling all mixed up, he gave up on sleep. At the moment he was anything but happy. He needed sex. The next best thing was exercise, followed by a long, cold shower.

A midnight run in the rain ought to do the trick. But with

Maggie asleep, leaving the house was out. He'd lift the weights he kept in a corner of the basement.

He threw on a T-shirt and gym shorts, laced up his sneakers and headed downstairs.

Chapter Five

Sunday night after G.G. was asleep, Tina sat at the kitchen table with her laptop, sketch pad and pencils spread out around her.

Except for the steady *tick, tick* of the wall clock in the living room and the hum of the refrigerator, the house was quiet. Perfect for catching up on all the work she'd neglected over the past few days. And there were piles of it. She'd been out of the office since Wednesday, and already she was woefully behind. Forget catching the interest of Peter Woods, the CEO of the Captain's Catch restaurant chain. She could barely stay on top of her regular responsibilities.

She was barely averaging six hours' sleep, but she was used to that. Besides, it was better to work late than toss and turn in bed, feeling sorry for herself. G.G. had raised her to focus on the positive, and Tina preferred not to think about loneliness or the fact that her life was sorely lacking in joy.

She prided herself on keeping her negative feelings well hidden. Yet somehow last night, Ryan had seen beneath the surface.

"You're not happy, either," he'd said.

The man was too darned astute. Tina fervently hoped that G.G. and the rest of the neighbors never realized how she felt. They wanted her to be successful, and her aim was to please them. That was what mattered.

Nothing to do but put on a convincing upbeat face and have a spring in her step every time she saw Ryan. Starting tomorrow night, when she stopped over to meet Maggie's hamster. Fooling him wouldn't be so difficult, as long as she focused on Maggie and her pet. And didn't think about wanting to kiss her daddy again.

Last night's kisses were still with her. If she closed her eyes, she could almost feel Ryan's lips moving restlessly over hers, hinting at untold pleasures and making her want much more. She thought about him lifting her and holding her tight against the hard planes of his body…

Her nerves began to thrum and sing. Ryan was so big and solid. Not much extra fat on his frame, as far as she could tell. She wouldn't mind finding out for sure, though.

Ryan without a shirt. At the very thought, her breath caught. Of course she would never see his bare chest, or even kiss him a second time. According to Ryan, it had all been a mistake.

No other man had ever apologized for a kiss. The laugh that broke from Tina's chest felt more like a cry. "I have sunk to new depths of humiliation," she murmured to herself.

She wished she hadn't agreed to come over tomorrow night. But she had, and Maggie expected her. To avoid being rude, she'd stay fifteen minutes, meet the hamster and then leave, wearing a huge smile on her face the entire time.

That settled, she focused on work. She was deep into an ad campaign for a microbrewery when her cell phone rang. The LED read, Kate and Jack Burrows. As busy as she and Kate both were, they still tried to talk every day.

Tina answered. "Hey, you."

"You sound sleepy. Am I calling too late?"

"Are you kidding? I was working. I'll be up for hours."

"Then I won't keep you long. How's G.G.?"

"Not great. But she did agree to see her doctor in the morning." Which was a huge relief.

"I sure hope you'll be able to come to Sam's party."

"You know G.G. She wants me to go, regardless, but I'd better wait until we see Dr. Dove. Can I let you know in a day or two?"

"No problem."

"I did sneak away during G.G.'s afternoon nap and bought Sam's Nerf tetherball set." It was a gift that Kate had mentioned her daughter wanted.

"She'll love it. Any news from work?"

"Yes, and it's infuriating." Though it was Sunday, Tina and June had talked a bit earlier, discussing ad campaigns and paperwork. "Wait until you hear what Kendra's been saying about me." Even talking about it upset Tina. Her stomach began to burn, and she fished the antacid bottle from her purse and popped a tablet. "According to her, now is no time to take my 'vacation.' She says I could easily hire someone to take care of G.G., and if I truly wanted the creative director job I'd be at the office, lobbying for it. In other words, she's spreading rumors that I'm not at all interested in the position."

"That bitch! What are you going to do?"

"I had planned to call Jim Sperling tomorrow morning and assure him that I definitely want the job. But instead, *he* called *me*." Right before G.G. had gone to bed. "He always says that family comes first. But I'm starting to wonder, since he set up my interview for *this* Thursday, instead of after Thanksgiving. Apparently, he wants to choose the right person before the holiday."

Tina's interview was four days from now. *Four days*, and she had yet to put together a proposal for the restaurant chain. The antacids weren't working, so she chewed another.

"Calling you on a Sunday? Making you come back and interview while G.G.'s sick and you're supposedly on vacation? Some family man. What are you going to do?"

"Go, of course." Tina sighed. "I don't want to leave G.G., but she insists. I'm thinking I'll fly over and back, as you suggested, to save time."

"Do you want me to stay with her while you're gone?"

Kate was so busy that Tina hated to bother her. "Let me check with the neighbors first, but thanks."

"Any time. I'll keep my fingers crossed, but there's really no need to. No matter what garbage Kendra's spreading, that job will be yours."

Maybe I don't want it. Given what Tina had just told Kate and what her loved ones wanted for her, it was a traitorous thought that she had no business entertaining. She shoved it away. "I appreciate the vote of confidence."

"Confidence, schmonfidence, you've earned the promotion. How was dinner last night?"

Tina wished she hadn't mentioned that to Kate, and wasn't about to share what had happened between her and Ryan. "It was okay, if you don't count G.G.'s obvious pain and Ryan's misguided concerns. He's worried that Maggie will get too attached to me and that she'll be hurt when I leave."

"That doesn't sound misguided to me."

"Come on, Kate, she knows I'm leaving after Thanksgiving. How attached can a child get in two weeks?"

"Good point—I guess."

"She did invite me to meet her hamster tomorrow night."

"How cute. I wonder if her father put her up to that."

Doubtful. "Ryan isn't interested, remember? And neither am I. I simply don't have time," Tina said, hoping she could convince both Kate and herself. "I should get back to work now, but I'll call you after G.G.'s appointment in the morning."

"I'd rather talk to you when you get back from the Chases' tomorrow night," Kate said. "Unless you're over there really late."

Tina dismissed her friend's suggestive comments by shaking her head at the ceiling. Which, of course, Kate couldn't see. "All right, but since I won't be there longer than fifteen minutes, you're going to be disappointed."

RYAN WASN'T in the best mood as he put away dinner leftovers on Monday night. Thanks to Maggie's nightmares, he was exhausted. And deeply troubled because throughout the day, even when they'd bought Sam's birthday gift, his daughter had talked nonstop about Tina.

She'd known the woman barely a week, but already she was way too attached. Not that Ryan blamed his daughter. He liked Tina, too. He'd sure enjoyed kissing her. In fact, since the other night, he'd thought about little else, and had fantasized about doing a whole lot more than just kissing her. Even dreamed about her—erotic things that left him frustrated and hungry.

Tough, because he wasn't doing a thing about it. Tonight, he'd be civil and nothing more.

If that wasn't enough, tomorrow was the first day of his bank's month-long promotion to bring in new deposits and loans. Without support from Corporate, keeping his staff pumped would be no easy feat, and Ryan dreaded what lay ahead.

While he loaded the dishwasher, he thought about the

Island Banking Corporation. Cheap bastards. The thing was, he loved banking. Just not *this* banking job. What he wouldn't give to start a new one and show them how a well-run bank operated.

But Maggie came first, and Ryan refused to waste any more time thinking about that challenge. It was either hold on to this job or find some other low-level position.

Dishes done, he riffled through the paper for the sports section, which he hadn't read yet. With Tina due any minute, he probably wouldn't be able to read much of it just now.

He owed her for pointing out that Maggie felt responsible for making him happy. All day he'd tried to joke around and pretend things were great, but lack of sleep and his mixed-up feelings for Tina had gotten in the way, and he'd done a lousy job. Lucky for him, today his daughter hadn't noticed his crappy mood. She was too excited about Sam's parties and Tina coming over tonight.

Suddenly Maggie showed up in the kitchen.

"Eggwhite wanted her cage to look pretty for Tina, so I cleaned it all by myself," she proudly announced.

"You did, huh?"

The cage was on the bookcase in her room, and Ryan's head filled with visions of wood chips and shredded newsprint littering the carpet. Tina would think he was a lousy housekeeper, though why he cared what she thought was beyond him. He eyed his daughter. "What did you do with the dirty shavings?"

She sighed like an adult answering a tiresome question. "Put it in the garbage can in the garage, just like always." She headed toward the refrigerator and opened it.

"Still hungry?"

"No, Daddy, I need lettuce for Eggwhite." She all but disappeared inside the appliance.

"Help yourself," he said, smiling to himself, since she already had.

When Maggie had her lettuce, she headed for the stairs. Newspaper in hand, Ryan trailed her as far as the living room. The doorbell rang, and she wheeled toward it.

"That's her! Tina's here, Daddy!" She shoved lettuce leaves at him, then raced for the door. Jumping up and down, she opened it. "Hi, Tina! Come in."

"Thanks."

Tina stepped inside, bringing a rush of cold and the scent of fresh air with her. She'd probably been outside all of a minute, but her cheeks were pink and she was slightly breathless. Her unpainted lips opened a fraction, the bottom one looking slightly chapped.

Nothing remotely sexy in that. But Ryan knew the taste of those lips. For all his resolve, he wanted to kiss her again. And more. Setting his jaw—he would be civil, period—he gave a terse nod. "Tina."

She pulled her lower lip between her teeth. She must've been doing that a lot lately. "Hello, Ryan."

Maggie stared up at her, too distracted to remember to close the door. Tina shut it, then slid a quizzical glance toward the lettuce in his hands.

"A treat for Eggwhite," he said, handing the greens to Maggie.

"Ah."

While Maggie carefully tucked the lettuce into the kangaroo pocket of her sweater and Ryan wiped his hands on his jeans, Tina glanced around the living room.

"I *knew* the walls wouldn't be pink anymore."

"First thing I changed after we bought the place."

"What an improvement. I like that shade of green."

She pulled a spike of hair through her fingers, then

fiddled with another, and Ryan could see that she was as uncomfortable as he was. For some reason, that only made him want her more.

Neither of them spoke until Maggie pulled on Tina's sleeve. "Don't you want to take off your coat?"

"I can't stay long."

That jibed perfectly with Ryan's plans, but he helped her out of her coat and hung it up anyway. "How's G.G. doing?"

"We saw Dr. Dove today." She bit on her lip again. "He says she's doing too much and should cut back, even with the physical therapy. He also wants her to follow up with her surgeon in Seattle, too, but she refuses to go all the way back there. She got Dr. Dove to call the surgeon and ask for the name of a doctor she could see in Anacortes. As soon as he calls with the information, I'll schedule an appointment."

Ryan studied his daughter, whose face had lost all traces of excitement. Not wanting her to worry, he ruffled her hair. "G.G.'ll be all right, Sunshine. Sometimes it just takes a while."

Tina nodded at Maggie and her face brightened.

"She's in bed now, but she promised to call if she needs help," Tina said. "How was your day, sweetie?"

"Awesome. We bought Sam's present. C'mon, I'll show you. But it's a surprise and you can't tell, okay?"

Tina's mouth twitched. "Girl Scouts' honor."

"We're keeping it in Daddy's study. This way."

Ryan's daughter scampered ahead, leading Tina into a small room across from the powder room. Ryan followed.

Maggie opened the closet and took out the shopping bag. "It's a My Little Pony purse!"

To Tina's credit, she managed to look impressed. "I love it."

His daughter broke into a grin. "Me, too. See Daddy, I

told you! Girls like stuff like this. He's gonna let me wrap it all by myself, aren't you?"

Ryan nodded. Time to show Tina the hamster and get her out of here. He opened his mouth, but Maggie spoke first.

"Look, Daddy!" She pulled out a bag full of jawbreakers. "We bought these at the store today. We forgot!" She chose one for herself, then held out the sack. "Want one?"

Tina shrugged. "Sure. Thanks."

The cellophane crinkled as she unwrapped her candy. Ryan took one, too. Sounds of pleasure issued from Tina's throat and her mouth made soft sucking sounds. From there, it didn't take much to imagine that mouth on him.

Did she have any idea what she was doing to him? Fortunately, Tina's attention was on Maggie.

"Let's go feed Eggwhite his lettuce," Maggie said, tugging Tina's hand. "You stay downstairs, Daddy."

Badly in need of space and a bit of time to corral his raging lust, Ryan didn't argue.

Giggling, Maggie pulled Tina toward the stairs.

As much as Ryan loved to hear that bubbling sound, the present cause of it bothered him. He watched them climb the stairs, his gaze drawn again to Tina's backside. She was wearing a hip-length maroon sweater and snug-fitting jeans.

Ryan's own jeans grew uncomfortably tight as he imagined placing his hands on her behind and pulling her against his body. Catching himself, he scowled. *Enough.* He headed for the sofa to read his paper.

But as he sank onto the cushions, Maggie shrieked, sounding extremely upset. Ryan dropped the newspaper, jumped up, and ran for the stairs.

"MY HAMSTER is gone," Maggie wailed.

Feeling helpless, Tina stood near the empty cage and

patted the child's quivering little shoulder while tears rolled down her face. The cage door stood open. Apparently, Maggie had forgotten to latch it.

Within moments Ryan strode into her room, as fierce as a warrior and ready to slay whatever dragons threatened his child. For that, Tina liked him even more.

"Daddy," she bawled, throwing herself against his legs.

After hugging her, he hunkered down and gently held her chin in one of his big hands. "What's the trouble, Maggie?"

"Look—no Eggwhite." Maggie pointed at the cage and sobbed.

Ryan seemed to know exactly what to do, holding his daughter close, one hand cupping her head against his chest, the other patting her back. "We'll find her," he said. "She can't have gotten far."

Despite his spoken assurances, he looked less than certain. Tina glanced around the room, with its white wood furniture, quilted pink bedspread and matching curtains, and shook her head in despair.

At last, Ryan held his daughter at arm's length. "Try to calm down, Sunshine, and let's get busy searching. I'll check the closet. What about you?"

Sniffling, Maggie turned toward her bed. "Maybe she's under the bed."

"Could be." Ryan glanced at Tina. "Why don't you look behind the dresser?"

Eager to help, Tina did. They spent a good ten minutes fruitlessly searching, before Ryan narrowed his eyes and stared at the wastebasket, which had fallen over. "Eggwhite loves paper. Why don't you check the trash, Maggie?"

The little girl pawed intently but carefully through a mass of wadded-up paper and tissues. Suddenly, the white hamster scrambled from under a scrap of construction paper. Ryan caught the small creature and returned it to its cage, and the bleak expression faded from Maggie's eyes.

With the dimple in Maggie's cheek once again winking, Tina felt as if a dark cloud had disappeared. No wonder Ryan worried so about her.

"This place is a mess," he said in a gentle voice Tina had never heard from him before. "I'll get the vacuum, and you and Tina feed Eggwhite that lettuce."

While he retrieved the vacuum, Tina returned the trash to the wastebasket and listened to Maggie scold her pet in loving tones.

"I'm glad you found her," she told Maggie.

"Me, too."

Ryan returned. "It's almost bedtime. I'll clean up, and you go brush your teeth and get ready for bed."

Without argument, his daughter headed for the bathroom.

It was nearly eight, and Tina had stayed far longer than she'd intended to. Time to go, but she couldn't leave without a good-night to Maggie. She waited until Ryan shut off the vacuum before speaking. "That was pretty emotional. Now I understand why…"

His attention jerked to the door. He shook his head in warning. An instant later, Maggie padded into the room.

She'd changed into a white flannel nightgown decorated with blue sheep. Her face was shiny and clean, and the pigtails were gone. So young to accomplish those bedtime tasks all by herself. But then, Tina, too, had grown up at an early age.

"That's a cute nightgown," she said.

"Thank you. Daddy let me pick it out. Will you button me?" She turned her back, lifting her hair and bowing her head.

The trusting act melted Tina's heart. She breathed in

Maggie's little-girl scent. Longing for a daughter of her own filled her so that her fingers trembled. "All done," she said in a shaky voice.

Maggie turned to her. "Tuck me in tonight, Tina."

Such a sweet, intimate request. As it was, Tina's emotions simmered dangerously close to the surface. And after what she'd just witnessed, she was afraid that regardless of her harmless intentions, Ryan was right—she would hurt the little girl when she left Halo Island.

"I'd better not," she said. "Isn't that your Daddy's job?"

"But I want you to. Daddy doesn't mind, do you?"

Looking as torn as Tina felt, Ryan blew out a heavy breath. "As long as you understand that Tina won't be here much longer. And that usually she visits the island only at Thanksgiving and Christmas." He paused and peered at her face. "Do you understand, Sunshine?"

"Yes, Daddy. I do."

He gave a terse nod. "All right. Do you want Tina to read the next chapter of *Beezus and Ramona?*"

"Uh-huh. You listen, too, Daddy." Maggie patted the bed beside her.

Tina brought a wooden, child-size chair from the table in the corner. She sat down near Maggie and opened the book. As she read, she felt the young girl's trusting eyes on her face. The way her own daughter would look at her, if she had one. What she wouldn't give for a family of her own. An ache filled her heart to breaking.

At last, Maggie's eyelids drooped. Ryan rose, and then carefully tucked the covers around her.

"Love you," he said, planting a kiss on her forehead.

"Love you," she echoed, before turning her head toward Tina. "I love you, too, Tina. You're my best new friend in the whole world."

"Aw." The backs of Tina's eyes stung, and she swallowed hard. "I love you right back."

Stern-faced, Ryan turned on the child's night light and turned off the bedside lamp. In silence, he and Tina headed down the stairs.

"Can you stay for a minute and talk?" he asked, gesturing toward the living room.

Feeling as raw as she did, she ought to go back to her room at G.G.'s and have a good cry. But God help her, she wanted Ryan's company. Was that so wrong?

Tina nodded and sat down.

Chapter Six

Earlier, Ryan had wanted Tina to leave. But now, with what had just happened… In her own innocent way, his daughter loved this woman, and Ryan was at a loss as to how to protect her from getting hurt. He hoped Tina had some ideas.

He sat down on a recliner across from the sofa, where Tina was seated. "You heard what Maggie said. As far as she's concerned, she loves you." Resting his hands on his thighs, he hung his head. "That's not good, not good at all."

"I'm very fond of her, too. She's such a special girl."

Eyes didn't lie, and Tina's were full of feeling. Ryan couldn't stop a smirk. "Yeah, but you're leaving." Like all the other women Maggie had loved and trusted. "What the hell am I supposed to do after you're gone?"

That day would come fast, all too fast. He thought he saw regret in Tina's face. Or was that his own wishful thinking?

"Without a mother's love, she'll gravitate toward any adult female who shows her genuine affection," Tina said. "That's what I did. How do you think I came to know G.G. so well? But Maggie also called me her friend, and she said she understood about my leaving. Maybe she really does and you're worried unnecessarily."

"I know my kid. No matter what she said tonight, when you leave, her heart will break. And dammit, there's not a thing I can do to stop it."

Eyes dark with remorse, Tina shook her head. "I'm sorry, Ryan."

He was, too. "'Sorry' won't make this any easier on her. You've walked in Maggie's shoes. Any ideas how to help?"

"Um, maybe a child psychologist?"

The thought of his daughter pouring her heart out to some neutral third party didn't sit all that well with Ryan. "No thanks. Any other suggestions?"

"Well, I know you don't want to hear this, but Maggie needs a mother."

As if he'd ever get married again. Liking this idea even less, he swore.

Tina winced. "I guess that's not what you wanted to hear. But it's the truth. She has all this love to give, and a deep yearning to feel a mother's love. That's why she used the L word with me."

Tina should know. It did make sense. For a second, Ryan wished he could go back in time and comfort the lonely child Tina had been. But hell, he couldn't even do that for his own daughter.

"Could be," he said. "But I'm through with marriage." He looked at her straight on, to make sure she heard him. "There'll be no mother for Maggie."

"Okay, then, what about a mother figure, a woman around my age, to spend quality time with her. It can't be me, of course, since I'm leaving…"

Her glum face told him that his hunch a second ago had been right, and she'd be sorry to leave Maggie. But Ryan was no fool. Once Tina got that promotion, she wouldn't have time to think about his daughter.

"There must be someone who lives in town who can become a regular part of her life," Tina said.

"You think there's a woman alive who'll hang out with us, knowing I'll never date her or put a ring on her finger?" Ryan scoffed. "Not very likely."

"You don't know if you don't look."

He wasn't about to do that. "Risk another attachment that ends with loss? No, thanks."

Tina let out an exasperated breath. "Why did you ask for advice, when you clearly don't want it?"

"I don't know." He scrubbed his face with his hands. "Damn, but I've made some bad choices with women. I've totally screwed up Maggie's life."

"Not with your wife. She *died*. That wasn't your fault."

"No, but we were talking divorce at the time. Heidi was too busy climbing the corporate ladder at her law firm to care much about Maggie or me. She never even wanted kids, but I pushed her to have a baby anyway. I thought it would bring us closer together." He snickered. "What a joke."

He'd never told anyone that before, and he couldn't believe he'd shared something so personal with Tina. By the look of her wide eyes, she couldn't quite believe it, either. God knew what she'd think of him now.

"Everybody makes mistakes, Ryan," she said, with a nonjudgmental tone that surprised him. "I certainly have."

"But your mistakes didn't hurt a helpless child."

"You're right, there. There are no children in my life."

Her melancholy smile confused him and made his chest ache. "Why so sad?" he said.

"Nothing important. Just think about the way you were with Maggie tonight—you're a wonderful father, Ryan."

"Then why is it she still has nightmares?" The anguish

evident in his own voice should have embarrassed him, but he was too distressed to care. "I've tried everything— talking them through and explaining that the monsters and bad people aren't real, promising to keep her safe, leaving the lights on. Nothing works."

"Hey, you." Suddenly, Tina was standing beside him, and resting her hand on his shoulder. "Don't beat yourself up about this."

Her touch reassured him and eased the tension that had tied knots in his muscles. He covered her hand with his own. And when she tried to move away, he kept hold of her. "Sit here." He pulled her onto the arm of the recliner.

She swiveled to face him, her eyes large and luminous. So beautiful that once again he lost himself in them. He cleared his throat. Let go of her hand. "Tell me about your interview. When is it?"

"This Thursday, which was totally unexpected. I've had to scramble to get help for G.G. The Rosses and Rose and Stanley and Norma have agreed to take turns and stay with her. She doesn't want that, of course. Says she can take care of herself. But she's too weak and in too much pain." She stared at her lap. "I really don't want to leave her, but she insists that I go. She's more excited about this opportunity than… Well, she can hardly stand it."

"And you? Are you excited?" he asked, truly curious to know.

"Not really. It's just an interview."

"Nervous?"

She shook her head. "My boss knows my work, and he knows me. But there are others who are just as qualified. One in particular, Kendra Eubanks. You never know."

"But you want that job, right?"

"Of course I do."

She stood and fingered the V-neck of her sweater, then sat down on the sofa again.

Ryan figured she must be worried about her competition. "You'll get it."

"What makes you think so?"

"You're smart and confident, and everyone on the island says you're great at what you do. And you want it. A boss can sense that hunger to get ahead."

"G.G. and the neighbors really want me to succeed."

She wouldn't meet his eyes. *Interesting.*

"And you don't?"

"I said I did." She crossed her legs. "How are things at the bank?"

"So-so." He told her about the deposit-and-loan promotion and his staff's low morale. "The fools at head office don't seem to understand that if their employees are unhappy, the customers will be, too."

"Sort of like Maggie being happy if you're happy."

"I guess."

He wanted badly to kiss the knowing slant right off her mouth. With effort he dragged his gaze away from those lips.

"You don't like working there, do you?"

"Not much," he said, before he could stop himself. "That's between you and me, and no one else."

"I won't say anything. But you don't need the money, so why don't you quit?"

"What would I do all day? Besides, I enjoy banking. My beef is with the Island Banking Corporation."

"What a shame there aren't other banks on the island."

"There would be, if I started another one."

A fantasy he'd kept to himself until now. Not only had he

shared that tidbit, but he'd revealed private information about himself and Heidi—and he'd admitted he disliked his job.

What had gotten into him tonight?

"That's a great idea," Tina said. "You certainly have the know-how to start another bank."

"Yes, but start-ups take a huge chunk out of your life, for months on end. I can't do that to Maggie."

Tina yawned, and Ryan glanced at his watch. Almost eleven. Nearly three hours had passed—a heck of a lot more time than he'd meant to spend with her.

"It's late," she said, standing. "We both need sleep."

Ryan stood, too—and thought about sleeping with Tina. But if that happened, lust would actually keep him up most of the night. Emphasis on *up*. He stifled a smile. With or without Tina in his bed, he was in for a restless night.

At the door, she turned to him.

"You should've seen your face when you mentioned starting a bank, Ryan. You lit up. Don't let go of what you really want. For you and for Maggie, be happy."

With her chin tilted and her eyes bright with conviction, she was irresistible. Powerless to fight his own instincts, he stroked her soft, warm cheek with his thumb. "Know what'd make me happy right now? Kissing you."

"I'd like that, too." Her eyelids fluttered shut. She leaned forward, raised her face and offered him her lips.

RYAN'S ARMS felt like heaven. Tina had known he'd wanted to kiss her for hours, since they'd first sat down to talk. She'd seen the desire in his eyes, and shared it.

This kiss was even better than the ones the other night, and when his lips demanded more, she opened her mouth and tangled her tongue with his. He tasted faintly of jawbreaker and man, a combination that only fueled her hunger for him.

She was wearing a V-neck sweater, and when he nuzzled and nipped the sensitive place at the crook of her neck she was glad she'd chosen it. Yearning to get even closer, she stood on her toes, grasped his shoulders and pressed against him. His chest was pleasantly hard against her breasts, and she felt his arousal against her hips.

Then, thank you, Lord, Ryan's hands were under the sweater. His palms slid up her back, bringing heat to her skin. When he reached her bra, he slid his fingertips across her rib cage, teasing the undersides of her breasts. Tina caught her breath, eased back ever so slightly and silently urged him to explore her breasts.

He cupped her gently, while his thumbs brushed her nipples. Pleasure shot through her and went straight to the apex of her thighs. Dampness pooled there, along with an aching need. Moaning softly, she arched her chest, thrusting her breasts more heavily into his hands.

Just when her knees threatened to buckle, it was over. Breathing hard, his eyes wild and hot, Ryan broke the contact. With unsteady hands, he pulled down her sweater.

"Good night, Tina, and good luck on Thursday."

Thursday? Oh, the interview. "Thanks," she managed. "'Night."

In a daze she headed back to G.G.'s house.

BY THE TIME the bank closed on Tuesday afternoon, Ryan was feeling as good as a man could, given that he was sexually frustrated and his daughter was suffering from nightmares. She'd had two bad dreams last night, no doubt triggered by Eggwhite's escape. Ryan hoped that with the hamster safe in her cage, Maggie would have an easier time tonight.

Nightmares aside, today he'd actually enjoyed his job.

The first day of the bank promotion had gone well. His staff had worked hard and brought in more new business than expected. That ought to please Corporate.

Now, with the doors closed, Ryan strode from his office, his footsteps echoing through the empty space. Serena and Danielle were counting money at their teller stations, which they'd decorated with cardboard turkeys and horns of plenty, in honor of Thanksgiving. Jason sat at his desk, filling out the usual reams of paperwork.

"Great job today," he told his employees.

All three of them looked pleased.

"Thanks to the signs and the newspaper ads, we sure were busy," Jason said. "For once, Corporate did something right."

Ryan had to agree. Island Banking Corporation had come through for them. But the credit for this first successful day belonged to his staff. "Advertising helped, but you three did the hard work. You're a crackerjack team, and I intend to let my superiors know just how valuable you are."

"They won't care." Danielle tucked her shoulder-length hair behind her ears and shrugged. "But I appreciate that you do." She nodded at the bowl of lollipops on the customer side of her teller window. "Want a sucker, Ryan?"

"Thanks." He helped himself.

"Hooray, I balanced," Serena said, loading her rubber-banded stacks of cash into a bag. "Did you and Maggie do anything special yesterday?"

"Just hung out together."

And after her meltdown, after she was asleep, the real fun had begun. Talking with Tina. Kissing and touching her, even though he knew better. Now he couldn't get the taste of her, the feel of her breasts, out of his brain. What was it about Tina Morrell that pushed reason and common sense straight out of his head? He wasn't about to analyze himself.

"Maggie's hamster escaped last night," he added. "Luckily we found it." He made a face, and his employees chuckled.

"That must've been awful," Serena said. "Ellie and Cameron share a guinea pig. If he got loose…" She shook her head. "It wouldn't be pretty."

"It was a mess," Ryan said. "You should have seen the carpet. I must've spent twenty minutes vacuuming."

He had meant to be funny. Instead, Serena and Danielle shot him pitying looks—a widower, raising his daughter alone. Ryan hated that. He and Maggie were doing okay. Except for the nightmares.

He glanced at his watch. "Time to go home. Are we ready to lock up?"

Five minutes later, they left the building. Thanks to the shorter number of daylight hours and the heavy rain clouds, the air was dark, cold and damp.

Traffic was light—nonexistent, compared to L.A.—and Ryan drove home on automatic pilot, his thoughts on Tina.

After what had happened last night, however, it was best to stick to his plan and steer clear of her. Between work, Maggie and Tina's upcoming job interview in Seattle, avoiding the woman shouldn't be difficult—at least until the weekend. By then, Ryan hoped he'd have a better grip on himself.

Meanwhile, he'd make sure to remind Maggie that Tina was leaving soon. If he repeated that often enough, it might sink in—with both of them.

He turned onto Huckleberry Hill Road. As he slowed to pull into his driveway, he couldn't help noting that G.G.'s living room and dining room were both lit up. The curtains were closed, though, and he couldn't see inside. He wondered whether the older woman felt better today, but figured he'd find out when he picked up Maggie from the Featherstones'. That was safer than calling Tina and asking.

He eased into the garage and killed the engine. As he strode toward the Featherstone house at the end of the cul-de-sac, he told himself that tonight he would not think about Tina at all. If Maggie mentioned her, he'd simply tune her out.

In no time at all, he'd move past this ridiculous infatuation.

Chapter Seven

"Brace yourself for a bumpy landing," D. J. Hatcher, the handsome thirtysomething pilot told Tina.

The small seaplane—she was the lone passenger—dropped lower over Lake Washington and headed toward a small airstrip at the edge of the water north of Seattle.

Tina tightened her seat belt, gripped the armrests and stared out her window. She was relieved to see that the cab she'd ordered was waiting. That would save precious time, and since she needed to stop by her apartment and change into a suit, and then meet with June before the interview, every minute counted.

The plane had left Halo Island before eight, and the hour-long flight had been noisy and choppy. Thank heavens she didn't have a queasy stomach. Burning, yes, and en route she'd popped an antacid and munched crackers in an effort to soothe her ulcer. She'd also used the time to look over her notes and prepare for her ten-thirty interview. Which, thanks to spending all her spare time working up ideas for Captain's Catch, she hadn't even thought about.

Despite D.J.'s warning, the plane set down smoothly. It taxied across the water toward the small terminal, and seconds later it rolled to a stop.

"That wasn't bad at all," Tina said.

"We got lucky," he quipped.

As far as she knew, D.J. had never crashed or caused his customers any harm, and she took the comment as a pilot's attempt at humor. As antsy as she was about the interview, she barely mustered a smile.

D.J. shut off the engine, then pulled off his earphones. In the sudden silence, Tina's ears rang. "Thanks, D.J." She unbuckled her seat belt, causing the pilot to shake his head.

"Don't get up just yet."

He slid from his seat and unlatched the door, his broad shoulders straining his chino shirt. He was an attractive man, but Tina's interests lay elsewhere. On Ryan. She hadn't seen him since Monday night—with G.G. to care for and everything else on her plate, who had time?—but she'd certainly thought about him. And the things he'd shared with her about his wife and his feelings about his job.

Most of all, his kisses and his hands on her breasts. Even now, as stressed as she was, her body hummed at the memory.

Don't start, she chided herself. With so much riding on her upcoming interview, she couldn't afford any distractions. Besides, what was the point of fantasizing? Ryan didn't want to start something with her—even if he *had* kissed her and more. She didn't want that, either. Really. Tina shifted in her seat. *Liar.* But what was, was, and G.G., Jefferson and the neighbors were counting on her to make them proud.

She watched as D.J. climbed down the ladder that led to the dock. The best thing for Tina was to ace the interview, get the promotion and immerse herself in work. In no time, she'd forget all about Ryan Chase. If she wanted a family of her own, she'd bury the urge for another few years—until she achieved more, career-wise, and satisfied the people who loved her.

As for Maggie… Tina wasn't sure what to do about her. If only she could do something to stop the nightmares and lift the burdens from those tiny shoulders. But she couldn't. Her best bet was to try to be Maggie's friend, no matter what happened with her father.

D.J. peered through the door. "All right, Tina, we're set now."

She grabbed her portfolio from the overhead bin and D.J. offered her a hand down.

"Good luck with that interview," he said.

"Thanks, and thanks again for the ride." After the interview, which wouldn't last more than ninety minutes, she'd return to the airstrip and fly back to the island. "What's the latest I can get here and still make the one o'clock flight?"

"Twelve forty-five," D.J. said. "See you then."

Buffeted by the chill wind, Tina hurried toward the cab. Her hair was a mess, and the weather had probably ruined her makeup, too. Well, she'd fix that at home.

The cab waited curbside while she dashed into her brick apartment building, quickly changed, made herself look professional and grabbed her mail. After a week at G.G.'s, her one-bedroom apartment felt empty and lonely, and Tina was glad to leave.

Twenty minutes later, her driver dropped her in front of the downtown high-rise that housed CE Marketing. The seventy-story structure stretched skyward, and a person couldn't even see the top floor, where CE Marketing was based, without craning her head back.

As Tina walked through the revolving doors, her mouth went dry and her stomach seemed to turn over. She swallowed hard and wondered whether she might be sick. She'd told Ryan she wasn't nervous about the interview, but she was.

After checking in with the security guard in the bustling lobby, she entered the elevator. During the trip up, she checked her hair and lipstick. Feeling reasonably ready, portfolio and coat under her arm, she exited. On the teak wall across the way, the sleek silver CE Marketing, Inc. sign greeted her. *It's showtime.* Doing her best to appear confident, smile firmly in place, Tina strode through the thick glass doors and into the familiar plush reception area.

The receptionist, a young redhead named Shelby, signaled her to wait while she deftly fielded phone calls. When she finished, she smiled. "It's good to have you back, even if it is only for the interview. How's G.G.?"

Tina wasn't surprised at the question. This sophisticated firm wasn't so different from small-town Halo Island, with most everyone knowing each other's schedules and projects.

"It's slow going," she said. "I've missed this place." Which was and wasn't true. "My interview isn't for another hour, but will you let Mr. Sperling know I'm here? And could you also ask June to meet me in my office?"

"Will do." Shelby spoke confidentially and crossed her fingers. "For the record, I don't believe a word Kendra's been saying. I'm rooting for you."

"Thanks."

Kendra's interview had taken place the day before, and according to June, she'd come out it of smug and self-assured. No telling what she'd said about Tina. Mad at her all over again, Tina walked down the hallway, her footsteps muffled by thick carpeting as she passed offices and looked in on faces she knew as well as her own. People greeted her with smiles, and many of them wished her good luck.

As Tina entered her office, June was waiting by the window. Her round face lit up. "You made it."

Her warmth eased Tina's jangled nerves. "It's good to see you," she said.

"And you." June's smile dimmed somewhat. "You haven't been eating or sleeping much, have you?"

Trust June to be candid—Tina valued that. She sighed. "I was sure my concealer would hide the circles. It's been a difficult week."

"I can't even imagine. Of course, with you gone, it hasn't been easy for me, either. Unlike you, I eat when I'm stressed, and since you left I must've gained ten pounds. If only I could give them to you."

Tina laughed. "I'm truly grateful for the extra time you've put in for me, and I'll make sure you're paid for every hour. I wish I could treat you to lunch today, but I have to hurry back to the island right after my interview. Let's schedule something after Thanksgiving?"

"It's a date."

Tina glanced at her watch. "We don't have much time, so we'd best get to work."

She sank onto her familiar office chair, glanced at her computer, fax and printer, and wheeled up to her expansive desk. The neatly stacked files and crowded in-box meant tons of work, which reassured her that regardless of whether or not she got the creative director title, she'd be too busy to think about Ryan. She *would*.

"What's with the long face?" Pulling up another chair, June sat beside her so that they both faced the desk. "Is anything wrong?"

"I was wondering how I'll ever get all this work done."

"You will."

They spent the next half hour reviewing files; Tina stacked those she'd take back with her.

Then Kendra strode in, her expensive suit and three-inch heels making her look like a model. "Well, well, look who came to work. Decided to finally show up and interview, did you?"

Tina looked Kendra right in the eye. "As you well know, a family member is sick, and I'm using up vacation time to care for her."

"Yes, and I'm *so* sorry."

"Actually, you're not," Tina challenged her. "You've been telling people, including Jim Sperling, that since I've taken time off I must not want this position. He doesn't believe you, of course." Tina hoped that was true. "And I don't appreciate the innuendo. You owe me an apology."

Kendra's eyes narrowed. Without a hint of remorse, she shrugged. "One does what one must. Good luck with the interview—you'll need it. Though frankly, I don't know why you're even bothering. The creative director spot is mine." She flipped her hair over a shoulder, pivoted toward the door and sashayed off.

"You told *her*," June said. "She must be really scared to grandstand like that. Don't let her intimidate you."

Believing that Kendra was every bit as qualified and talented as she was, Tina *was* unnerved. Not about to show it, she smiled. "My track record speaks for itself. I'm not worried."

"That's my Tina."

The intercom buzzed. Tina reached for it. "Let me," June said, pushing the button. "Yes, Shelby?"

"Tell Tina that Mr. Sperling is ready for her."

"Will do. Thanks." June shut off the intercom. "You heard the lady. Go get 'em, kid." She gave Tina a thumbs-up.

Tina freshened her lipstick and fluffed her hair. Then she stood and straightened her suit jacket. "How do I look?"

"Like the next creative director."

Shoulders squared, knowing she looked calm and assured, she headed toward her boss's office. Inside, she felt nervous and confused, and not at all certain she wanted the position. But for G.G. and the others, she would do her best to get it.

FOR NEARLY TWO HOURS, Tina had faced Jim Sperling across the table in his private conference room, and still the meeting went on. She was due at the airstrip in twenty-five minutes, and she couldn't miss the flight. *Hurry up,* she silently pleaded.

In her opinion the interview had gone well and had been more like a conversation between fellow advertising professionals than the back and forth question-and-answer ordeal she'd anticipated.

Wearing a hand-tailored suit, crisp shirt and tasteful silk tie, with his silver hair expensively styled, Jim Sperling certainly looked the role of successful CEO. He nodded at her portfolio. "I like your plans for Captain's Catch," he said, acting as if he had all the time in the world to talk business with her. "It shows great initiative, but then time and again you've proved that you're ambitious. When do you plan to contact Peter Woods?"

"As soon as I get back—the Monday after Thanksgiving."

Her boss looked suitably impressed. Tina gave herself a pat on the back and waited for him to wrap up the meeting. But he said nothing. She had no choice but to take charge.

"Thank you so much for giving me a chance to interview for the creative director job."

"I'd have been surprised if you hadn't wanted to."

"I've taken up enough of your time, Jim. And I need to catch a plane back to the island soon."

His slightly narrowed eyes worried her.

"Right." He pushed back his chair and stood.

"This *is* my vacation," she reminded him.

"I'm well aware of that, Tina." Turning his back on her, he moved toward the closed door.

Stomach churning, she followed. Had she blown the interview by ending it herself, rather than waiting for him? *Of course not.*

"Please give G.G. my wishes for a speedy recovery," her boss said, opening the door.

"I will, and I'll definitely be back the Monday after Thanksgiving, ready to give the job my best."

He gave a curt nod. "Family's important, but of course so is CE Marketing."

The tension radiating from the man was disturbing, and this was no way to leave things. "Thanks again for interviewing me," Tina said, smiling and holding out her hand. "So I'll know whether I got the job before Thanksgiving?" When setting up the interview, he'd said as much. Since today was Thursday and the company closed at five o'clock tomorrow for the entire week of Thanksgiving, that meant she'd hear by tomorrow afternoon.

His face gave away nothing. "I'll make my decision fairly soon."

Whatever that meant.

"When I do," Jim Sperling said, "I'll be in touch."

RYAN ENJOYED Saturdays. He and Maggie slept in and he cooked a real breakfast instead of just pouring cold cereal into bowls. This morning, the smells of coffee, bacon and pancakes filled the kitchen. After a bad night—Maggie had cried herself and her father awake several times—they especially needed a pleasant breakfast.

Ryan had been certain that with Eggwhite caged and safe, his daughter would sleep better. Not so, however, and he felt powerless to help her.

Hell. Maybe Tina was right, and he should take her to a therapist.

His own sorry state was not terrific, either. He hadn't seen Tina since Monday night. He'd wanted it that way and had meant to get a grip on his undeniable feelings for her. But on his way home from work last night, Norma had called to let him know that she and Maggie were at G.G.'s, and to pick up Maggie there. Knowing he should avoid Tina, Ryan had knocked on the door with way too much anticipation. But she wasn't there. She'd taken advantage of Norma's visit to run to the pharmacy for more pain pills.

His keen sense of disappointment bothered him, and he acknowledged the fact that he hadn't corralled his desire at all. If he could just forget the taste of her mouth and the feel of her body against his….

Scowling, he flipped a batch of pancakes. Lately, he'd worked out so much that his muscles ached, and he was getting pretty sick of cold showers.

According to G.G., Tina hadn't heard about the job yet, but she thought the interview had gone well. Above all else, she wanted a career, and Ryan had best remember that. And he would get through the next week without touching her—or die trying. He set his jaw. Come next Sunday, she'd be gone. Out of sight, out of mind, he told himself, forgetting that the strategy hadn't worked over the past four days.

Until next Sunday he'd continue to remind Maggie—and himself—that Tina was about to leave. With luck, by the time Christmas rolled around, Maggie would be fine and he'd be back to his normal self, a man who resorted to occasional encounters with women who wanted what he did—mutual gratification and nothing more.

He was cooking the last batch of pancakes when his daughter bounded into the kitchen, robe flapping behind her.

"Hi, Daddy! Mmm, mmm, it smells good in here."

Whatever haunted her in dreams was gone now. Relieved, he ruffled her hair. "Morning, Sunshine. Ready for breakfast?"

"Yes!" Moving away she climbed into her chair. "What're we having?" She reached for the glass of orange juice Ryan had set out for her.

"Your favorite—pancakes and bacon."

"Yummy!"

"How many pancakes do you want?"

"Five, because I'm five! And one piece of bacon, please."

Ryan doubted she'd eat more than three pancakes, but this was supposed to be a happy breakfast, so what the heck? "Coming right up."

He filled her plate and set the food in front of her. Then he served himself half a dozen pancakes and four strips of bacon. After helping Maggie with maple syrup and cutting up her food, he smiled.

"Let's make a toast," he said with a nod at her milk glass. He'd introduced her to toasts on her birthday the previous August. He raised his coffee cup.

"Oh, goody!" Looking intent and serious and very grown-up, Maggie copied the gesture, using both hands to lift her milk.

"To a great day," Ryan said. *And a night free of scary dreams.*

Maggie clinked her glass against his cup, and they both sipped.

"Can I make a toast, too, Daddy?"

A thin line of milk coated her upper lip. Ryan resisted the urge to wipe it off until after this next toast. "Sure."

"I get to go to Sam's birthday party today and wear my princess dress. Yay!" Chortling, she again clinked rims with Ryan.

Not exactly a toast, but the giggles filling the room gladdened his heart.

"Can we do it again?" Maggie asked, after all but draining her glass.

Ryan swiped her mouth with his napkin. "Better not, or our food will get cold. Let's eat."

As he'd predicted, his daughter left half her breakfast. When she was done, he scooped the leftovers onto his plate and finished them.

"Can I go see G.G. and Tina this morning?" Maggie asked.

"In your pajamas?" he teased.

"No, silly. After I get dressed."

Yesterday G.G. had looked terrible—thin, her face taut with pain and nearly gray. Ryan wondered whether Tina had scheduled an appointment with a doctor in Anacortes and when that would happen. Unless the appointment was today, he thought Tina should take her back to the clinic.

"You saw G.G. yesterday," Ryan said. "Her hip hurts and she needs to rest. Besides, we have chores to do. It's cleaning day, remember? We want to finish in time for Sam's party." Which started at two. "And you need time to wrap her present."

"I know that, Daddy." Maggie's little mouth tightened into a stubborn line. "But I made G.G. a get-well card last night. Can't I please bring it to her? Then she'll feel better. I promise not to stay."

The card was news to Ryan. "That's really thoughtful, Sunshine. We'll stick it under her welcome mat. Right now, though, it's time to get dressed." Hoping that would be the end of the matter, he stacked the dishes, slid back his chair and stood up.

"I could give it to Tina."

"She's busy with G.G. You don't want to bother her."

"'Kay." Maggie gave an adult-size sigh. "Hey, maybe she'll drive me to Sam's party."

"She may not even go." Her stricken look tugged at his heart. "If G.G.'s feeling bad, Tina will want to stay home with her."

"Okay, but Tina knows how to do hair. If I'm a really good girl and get my chores done, can she fix my hair for the party?"

"I'm sick of hearing about Tina. Please, stop talking about her!"

At his sharp tone, Maggie's face darkened. "I thought you liked her."

The last thing he needed was to upset his daughter. He tucked her hair behind her ears. "First of all, you're always good, Sunshine. Second, I *do* like Tina." They both did, way too much. That was the problem. "Remember, she's leaving next weekend."

"I know. Don't be sad, Daddy." Maggie patted his leg. "It'll be okay. If you want, I'll stay home from the party so you don't get too lonesome."

She still felt responsible for his happiness, and his short fuse wasn't helping. Ryan lightened his expression. "Hey,

I'm not lonesome, I'm fine. But if you stay home, *that*'ll make me sad."

She looked doubtful, so he crossed his eyes, put out his tongue, fixed his thumbs in his ears and wiggled his fingers. "See?"

Maggie giggled, and Ryan blew out a relieved breath.

"If we don't start our chores, they'll never get done." He gently pointed her toward the doorway. "You get dressed while I clean up the kitchen. Then we'll tackle your room."

Chapter Eight

"Are you sure about this?" Tina asked G.G., who lay on the sofa. Her face was ashen, and clearly she still was in so much misery that Tina wasn't at all sure she should go to the birthday party. "I'm happy to stay home. Kate and Sam will understand."

"Nonsense. That party will take your mind off the promotion." G.G. gave her an anxious look. "I just wish Mr. Sperling would call."

"I'm not worried," Tina said.

Which was a lie, but G.G. was already concerned enough without worrying over Tina. Jim Sperling was not a man to take his time making decisions, though, and Tina feared that she'd blown it, after all, and he'd chosen someone else for the job. If that happened, G.G. and everyone would be *so* disappointed. The very thought made Tina feel queasy, yet she managed a reassuring smile.

"Look." G.G. gestured at the front window. "I see Marty and Susan Ross coming up the walk. So go and have fun."

The doorbell rang, and Tina let them in.

"Hi, G.G., and hello, Tina." Susan gave Tina a brief hug. "That's a pretty outfit. Isn't it a lovely afternoon?"

At some point overnight or early that morning the rain

had stopped and the clouds had vanished, making a welcome change in the weather.

Marty followed, with another hug. "Hi, honey. Afternoon, G.G." He hung up his and Susan's coats. "You up for a game of Scrabble this afternoon, G.G.?"

"I don't think so."

Her failure to put on a cheerful face around company, something she otherwise always managed, made Tina uneasy. "I'm staying home," she said.

"Absolutely not." G.G. set her jaw. "Help her with her coat, will you, Marty? It's the beige one."

He took Tina's coat from the closet and held it up for her. "She'll be okay without you," he said.

"All right, but I'll leave my cell on—so call if you need anything."

Filled with misgivings, Tina picked up Sam's brightly wrapped tetherball set and stepped outside. Marty closed the door behind her. The sunlight felt good on her face, and she drew in a breath of cold, fresh air and released it.

Aside from a dog barking somewhere in the distance and the occasional sounds of distant cars on Treeline Road, all was quiet. So different from her noisy Seattle neighborhood. Tina hardly knew her neighbors there—another big difference.

She headed along the stone walkway toward her car, which was parked in front of the carport. On the way, she glanced at Ryan's house. She hadn't seen him since Monday night. The front drapes were open. Tina quickly shifted her gaze—in case someone was looking out. Not that that was likely, this being the day father and daughter did their weekly cleaning. Actually, with the party starting soon, Maggie probably was upstairs getting ready.

Tina had enjoyed the little girl's visit late yesterday afternoon, and had been both sorry and relieved that she'd arrived home from the trip to the pharmacy after Ryan had picked her up. Sorry because she liked the man, and relieved for the same reason. She liked him way too much, and could easily fall for him.

A man who didn't want love or a relationship. Which really was for the best, since her life and her work were in Seattle.

Still, feeling as she did, with the memory of Ryan's sizzling kisses so fresh in her memory, it was best to see as little of him as possible. She was only here for another week. Unless G.G. stayed this sick, and Tina didn't want to think about that. Surely by next Sunday she'd feel better. Regardless, aside from Thanksgiving dinner, to which Ryan and Maggie were invited, she would avoid him. When she did see him, she'd be friendly but distant. Nothing more. By the time they gathered again at G.G.'s for Christmas dinner—no doubt Ryan and Maggie would be invited—she'd be completely over him.

She reached around the unwieldy package to open the back door of her sedan. At the same time, Ryan's front door opened. Maggie spilled through it and skipped across the big porch. Behind her, his face dark and unreadable, Ryan followed. Tina's heart gave a joyous thump.

Maggie spotted her and her face lit up, as bright as the sunshine. "Hi, Tina!" she shouted.

Pigtails flying, she bolted toward the street. At Ryan's warning, she stopped to wait for him. He took hold of her hand, but still she tugged him forward, a tiny powerhouse pulling the reluctant full-sized male in her wake.

Tina set Sam's present on the backseat. When she straightened up, Ryan was standing before her. It had been only four days, but she'd missed him. Oh, she had it bad.

She tried to quiet her thudding heart with a deep breath. *Friendly but distant*, she reminded herself. "Hello, Ryan."

"Tina."

The pleasure shining in his eyes was at odds with the tense set of his jaw, and she knew he remembered the other night as vividly as she did.

He glanced toward the house. "How's G.G. today?"

"Not so good."

"She looked like hell yesterday. When is that doctor's appointment?"

"I couldn't get her in until the day after Thanksgiving."

"If I were you, I'd take her back to the clinic."

"Believe me, I've suggested that more than once. But you know how stubborn she is. She won't go back."

Ryan made a sound of disapproval, and Tina glared at him. "I can't exactly force her, can I? At least she's following Dr. Dove's advice and resting more. And she doesn't have a fever. I check every night."

"Is G.G. gonna die?" Maggie asked. Her eyes were round and dismayed.

"Of course not, sweetie. She'll be fine." *Eventually.* Tina forced a smile. She noted the gauzy ankle-length pink dress under Maggie's parka and her pink patent leather shoes. "Don't you look pretty."

The little girl perked up. "This is my princess dress, the one I got for Halloween. Only I changed my mind and didn't wear it then, so Daddy said I could today. Watch me." Maggie twirled around, the skirt billowing out. "Do I look like a princess, Tina?"

"You certainly do. A beautiful one."

"Is that Sam's birthday present?" Maggie said, eyeing the package in Tina's car.

Tina nodded. "I was just leaving for her party."

She'd thought about offering Maggie a ride, but hadn't wanted to see Ryan. Then there was the other problem— Maggie was too attached. Well, so was Tina. And it was too late now. "Would you like a ride?"

"Can I, Daddy?"

Ryan shook his head. "I'm going out anyway, Sunshine, and I want to wish Sam happy birthday. I'll drive you."

"Then Tina can come with us, right?"

And make things even more awkward? She shook her head. "That's very sweet of you, but I don't think—"

"No sense both of us using up gas," he said, looking trapped. "You may as well ride with us."

Maggie jumped up and down. With no way out, Tina retrieved Sam's gift. *Friendly but distant,* she silently repeated, and they crossed the street to Ryan's car.

"OH, I LOVE birthday parties," Maggie sang from the backseat, making up the tune and the words as Ryan turned onto Treeline Road.

From time to time she kicked the back of the driver's seat, unable to contain her enthusiasm. Birthday parties always put her in high spirits, and Ryan was glad she'd spend the afternoon with her friends instead of worrying about him. Add Tina beside him in the passenger seat, and his daughter was riding high.

How the hell was he going to patch up her heart after Tina left? he wondered for the millionth time. Tina seemed worried about that, too—at least he figured that was the reason she was subdued. That and concern for G.G.

"Aren't you excited, Tina?" Maggie asked.

Tina glanced over her shoulder and smiled. "I certainly am."

Then she returned her gaze to whatever was out her

window—the nearly bare trees, blue skies and houses. Leaving Ryan with a great view of her slender neck.

She must've felt his gaze, for she glanced over at him, blushed and looked away. But not before he noted the warmth in her eyes.

Desire rolled through Ryan. He was sick to death of wanting her, but his body didn't care. Mouth tight, he shifted in his seat.

Fog clouded the front window, and he turned on the defroster and focused on driving. Yet all the while he was keenly aware of the subtle coconut scent that came from her hair.

"Eggwhite says she's sorry she ran away the other night," Maggie said.

"I know she must be." Tina twisted around to talk with Maggie.

She'd slipped off one shoe. Why that turned him on was anybody's guess. And sitting beside her was agony.

"We're here." He signaled and turned. Seconds later, he rolled up the driveway and braked to a stop behind two other cars.

Giggling and bouncing, Maggie unfastened her seat belt. She grabbed Sam's gift, which she'd wrapped all by herself. Despite the heavy use of tape, wrinkled corners and lopsided bow, she seemed proud of what she'd done. That was all that mattered.

Ryan popped the trunk so that Tina could get her gift, then slid out his side and opened the back door. Maggie hopped out, and Ryan bent down to give her pigtails a playful tug. "Have fun, Sunshine. I'll be back to get you later."

"I thought you were coming inside to wish Sam happy birthday."

Tina stood behind his daughter, her eyebrows arched slightly.

Right now, he wanted only to put some distance between himself and Tina. "I'll do that when I pick you up, all right?"

Maggie nodded. She gave his cheek a hasty peck, then pulled away. "'Bye, Daddy."

With eyes that glowed, she grabbed Tina's hand.

His daughter was crazy about Tina. That scared Ryan witless, and kept him from wondering whether he, too, might be falling for her.

TINA HADN'T BEEN to a family birthday party in years, not since moving away from the island. Now, sharing the afternoon festivities with Kate, Jack, their kids, parents, other relatives and friends, she was glad G.G. had pushed her to attend.

Standing in Kate's bright, modern kitchen, taking ice cream from the freezer while Kate stuck candles in the cake and her mom carried plates and utensils into the dining room, listening to the sounds of people laughing and chatting at the table, Tina shook her head. "This is some cool party. Now I know what I've been missing all these years."

"I'm so glad you made it." Kate smiled warmly. "Now that you know what it's like, maybe you'll find a way to come back for the next one."

"That would be nice." Tina made a silent pact with herself to do just that. "It's been great, visiting with Jack and the kids, and your parents. And Paul." Kate's older brother. "His wife seems wonderful, and their kids are so cute."

She envied the love that flowed openly among the family members. Maybe someday… "You're so lucky," she said.

"I know." Kate let out a happy sigh and lit the candles. "Come on, let's bring out the cake and ice cream."

After everyone enjoyed dessert, they gathered in the family room, where Sam tore open her gifts, crowing over every one. She loved the change purse Maggie had given her, and clipped it to the sash around her waist. As she peeled paper from the Nerf tetherball set, she squealed—something all the little girls seemed good at.

"Thank you, Tina!" She blew kisses Tina's way.

Pleased, Tina grinned. "You're very welcome."

Once the gifts had all been opened, the games began. A treasure hunt kicked off the fun, followed by pin the ponytail on the girl. Then they lined up for a chance to break open the pink pony piñata that hung from the ceiling of the back porch. Inside the piñata were toys and candy, and all the children were eager to break it open.

Tina helped, blindfolding and gently spinning the children one by one before they lurched forward, waving a plastic baseball bat in the air and hoping to connect with the piñata. Each got three tries. Though highly stimulated, they were remarkably patient while they waited their turns. Maggie was so excited, she danced her way forward.

Tina fitted the blindfold around her eyes. "Can you see anything, Maggie?"

She shook her head. "Spin me, Tina."

Tina turned her around several times, then released her. "Go get 'em, kiddo."

On the first two tries she missed, but on the third the bat connected with the piñata. A loud *crack* filled the room, and the kids went wild, jumping up and down and shouting.

"You did it, Maggie!" Tina pulled off the blindfold. "Hooray!"

The beaming child threw her arms around Tina. "I love you, Tina."

Hearing it for the second time felt as good—and as heart-wrenching—as before. Tina held her tight. "I love you, too." For Maggie's sake and her own, she added, "It'll be sad when I leave next Sunday, won't it?"

Maggie nodded solemnly and Tina squeezed her shoulder.

Though she never could be more than a friend to the girl, she couldn't help pretending, just for the rest of the party, that Maggie was hers and that she, Maggie and Ryan were a family. A far-fetched fantasy, but as long as no one but she knew, where was the harm?

By the time Ryan walked into the house to pick them up and wish Sam a happy birthday, Tina felt hollow inside. She managed to laugh and act as if she were having a terrific time, but the truth was, she'd never felt so lonely.

She understood, then, that her dream of Ryan and Maggie as her ready-made family wasn't harmless, at all. She had the empty heart to prove it.

Chapter Nine

As Tina tucked G.G. in Monday night, she frowned at the new lines etched into the woman's colorless face. "Maybe we should call off our Thanksgiving dinner this year."

"And let those lovely people down? Nonsense. Besides, it's not for another three days. By then, I'll be fine."

Tina had her doubts. "You need rest," she said. "They'll understand if we cancel."

They being Jefferson Jeffries, Ryan and Maggie. The rest of the neighbors celebrated the holiday with their own relatives.

"Tina Morrell, you know perfectly well that I always host Thanksgiving and Christmas dinner." G.G.'s lips compressed into a stubborn line. "I'm not about to let this stupid hip get in my way. Besides, you're doing all the work. My only job will be to make out the grocery list. The stuffing, pie making and everything else is up to you."

Which was a lot of work. "All right." Tina sighed. "But I don't know if the meal will turn out as well as yours always does."

"Of course it will. All the recipes are in the box I keep with the cookbooks."

Suddenly, Tina's cell phone rang.

"Is it Mr. Sperling?" G.G. asked, looking hopeful.

"I doubt it." For G.G.'s sake, Tina made sure she looked cheerful and sounded upbeat. "He wouldn't call this late in the day," she said, fairly certain he wouldn't call at all. The offices were closed now, and she assumed she and everyone else would find out who'd been named creative director next Monday.

She slid her phone from her sweater pocket and looked at the LED. "It's Kate. Hey, you," she said in greeting.

"Hi, Tina. I need a favor." Kate's voice was so weak and scratchy, Tina could barely understand her.

"You sound awful. What happened to your voice?"

"Laryngitis and a bad cold. I sure hope you and everyone else who came to the party stay well. Hold on a sec." Though Kate covered the phone, Tina heard her hacking cough. "I'm back," she croaked. "Listen, I'm supposed to help Sam's class with a field trip tomorrow. Is there any chance you could go in my place?"

"Me?"

"It was Sam's idea. She had such fun with you at her party. If you say yes, I'll let Mrs. Jenkins know. All you have to do is show up in the classroom at nine forty-five and drive four of the kids in your car. You'll be home by noon."

"Give me a minute to think."

"Okay. I'll use the time to blow my nose."

Tina knew she could ask someone from the neighborhood to stay with G.G. She thought about Maggie, who was in Sam's class. Spending a few hours on a field trip in her company appealed to Tina. Plus, she was tired of working every spare minute—especially now that she knew the promotion would go to someone else.

"What's wrong, dear?" G.G. asked.

Tina placed her hand over the mouthpiece of the phone.

"I'm listening to Kate sniffle and cough. She's really sick. Would you mind if I helped her out in the morning and went with Sam's class on a field trip? It's only for a few hours, and I'm sure one of the neighbors will be happy to come over."

"Go right ahead."

"I'm back," Kate rasped.

"It's okay with G.G., so yes, I'm happy to help out." G.G. gave a feeble smile, and Tina returned it. "It'll be fun."

"Find out more about the field trip," G.G. said.

"Just where are we going?"

"Well, um, Halo Island Bank."

"The bank?"

G.G.'s eyes glinted. "You'll get to see Ryan at work."

Tina scoffed. "Oh, that'll be fun."

Yet her spirits lifted with anticipation. Not a good thing. She thought about backing out, but she'd already agreed to go.

Besides, with twenty kindergartners to watch over, she'd be way too busy to moon over Ryan.

SITTING AT HIS DESK, Ryan scrubbed his hands over his face. Of all the days for a kindergarten field trip. Today marked the end of the first week of the bank's promotion, and though he was pleased with the efforts of his staff, the numbers weren't as good as Bernard Beale, chairman of the Island Banking Corporation, wanted. Without so much as a nod to everyone's hard work, Beale had sent out a be-littling company-wide e-mail, threatening pay cuts and possible dismissals for those he described as "employees who didn't carry their weight."

Ryan was outraged, and if the kindergartners weren't

due any minute, he would have phoned Beale with a few nasty comments of his own. After the kids left, he'd contact Beale and let him know just how far off the mark he was. Not that that'd change anything. His staff knew it, too, and they all were demoralized. Man, did he hate his job today.

But now was no time for a bad mood. In a few minutes his daughter and her class would troop through the door, and his first priority was to make their field trip fun. Danielle had the day off. Ryan headed for Serena's teller window and gestured Jason over. Both employees looked glum.

"I know this morning started badly, but Maggie's class will be here soon," Ryan said. "Let's give them a fun experience."

"This place, fun?" Serena's lip curled. "Ha!"

"It's not the kids' fault that Corporate treats us like crap," Jason said. "I guess we can try."

"I'd appreciate that." Ryan scrutinized the lollipop bowl, which was half-empty. He wanted each of the kids to leave with one. "Do you need to run to the store and pick up more lollipops?"

Serena shook her head. "I've got plenty more back here. I'll fill the bowl." She did, shaking her head. "With all those kindergartners, it's going to be noisy and crazy in here."

This morning Ryan wanted that. A bank full of energetic kids might lighten the gloomy atmosphere. He shared his ideas for showing the kids around, with Serena and Jason each taking half of the group to the vault and behind the teller windows. Ryan would show them his office and explain a few basics about bank accounts.

At ten-fifteen they marched in, twenty kids, Mrs. Jenkins and several parents Ryan recognized. Maggie was one of the first through the door, flanked by Sam and Gina, her two best friends.

When she spotted Ryan, she shrieked. "Daddy!" She flew at him for a quick hug. "Look who came with us—Tina!"

She was right behind his daughter, and the last person Ryan had expected to see. He didn't like the sudden lift of his spirits or the extra warmth he felt in his chest. Yet, despite the curious stares of Jason, Danielle and the rest of the adults in the lobby, he couldn't tear his gaze from her or stop himself from moving closer.

The cold had put roses in her cheeks and the wind had whipped her hair, making it spikier than usual. She looked beautiful. Her eyes held his and flashed with pleasure, as if she was equally pleased to see him. That made him feel good, until he realized how crazy this was. *She's leaving Sunday, remember?*

"What are you doing here?" he asked, aware that he sounded brusque, but not caring.

Startled, she stepped back, her expression instantly closing off. "Kate Burrows was supposed to help, but she's sick. Sam asked if I could go in her place, and here I am."

Without the light in her eyes, she looked drawn and tired. Ryan figured G.G. must not be any better. He would ask about that later. Everyone was busy taking off coats and piling them on the lobby chairs.

"It's not the best day for a field trip," he told Tina in a low voice. "Corporate's giving us crap for… Never mind. This isn't the time or place. Any word on your job?"

"Not yet." She sighed. "The offices are closed this week, and I should've heard by now. I don't think I got it." She dug into her purse and pulled out a bottle of antacids. Ate one. "G.G. and the others will be so upset. Please don't say anything."

"I won't. But hey, it ain't over yet. No news could be good news. What about you? Will you be upset if you don't get the job?" he asked, pretending he didn't care.

She looked at him as if he'd grown six ears. "What kind of question is that?"

Ryan had to agree. And wondered why he'd asked.

The coatless kids and adults gathered around, and he started his spiel. "Welcome to Halo Island Bank. I'm Ryan Chase, the branch manager."

"That's my daddy," Maggie said, clearly proud.

If she only knew how angry he was—and how unhappy.

"This is a small bank, with just myself and three employees," he said. "One of the tellers, Danielle, has the day off. But Jason and Serena—" he nodded at them "—will show you around."

"Tina, you come with Sam and Gina and the rest of my group," Maggie said.

She nodded and headed off.

Ryan watched her. She was a natural with kids, treating them with warmth and affection. She'd make some kid a great mom. Now, that was a joke. Tina wanted a big career, not marriage and motherhood.

Later, as the teacher and parents lined up the class and herded them toward the door, Ryan fell into step beside Tina. "What about Thanksgiving? Is G.G. well enough?"

"No, but she won't let me cancel."

Fool that he was, he was glad. "What should we bring?"

"A sweet potato dish. We're eating at three."

"We'll be there."

As Tina slid two pumpkin pies into the oven Wednesday evening, her cell phone rang.

Hastily wiping her hands on a towel, she slipped it from her pocket and glanced at the LED. *Jim Sperling*.

Heart in her mouth, she answered. "This is Tina," she said in a voice she hoped sounded cool, yet professional.

"Jim Sperling here."

"Who are you talking to, Tina?" G.G. called from the den. After her nap she'd stayed in bed, which was worrisome.

"Would you excuse me a moment?" Tina covered the mouthpiece with her hand. "It's Jim Sperling."

"Oh, my goodness."

Thankful she wasn't in the den, where G.G. would scrutinize her every expression, Tina dropped into a kitchen chair. "Okay, I'm back."

"All ready for Thanksgiving?"

"Almost." *Get to the point, get to the point.* "How about you?"

"Marian has been slaving away for days. How's G.G.?"

"Not great, but she's seeing a doctor on Friday." Tina fervently hoped that Dr. Lomax, the doctor in Anacortes, could figure out how to fix G.G.'s hip troubles. Otherwise…

"I assume you have a caregiver lined up for next week and that you'll be back Monday?"

Tina hadn't even considered bringing in an outsider. But G.G. was too ill to be looked after by her neighbors, and with Tina's "vacation" over, she probably *should* find someone. The very idea went against the grain—*she* should care for G.G. "I'm working on that," she said.

"Good. Now, the reason for my call. I have wonderful news, Tina. It was a tough decision, but I've made up my mind. The creative director position is yours."

"Really? That's wonderful news!"

She knew she sounded excited and pleased enough. If

she *felt* nothing, that was most likely because she was in shock. Not because she wanted what no job could provide—a family of her own—but because she'd truly believed that someone else would get the promotion.

For several moments she just listened to her boss, trying to remember to comment when expected.

"The job starts Monday," he said. "I want to make the announcement first thing that morning, and I expect you to be there."

"I'll be in by eight," she promised.

"Congratulations, Tina," her boss said. "Please give G.G. my regards."

"I will. Thank you so much, Jim."

Her mind in a whir, she headed for the den.

G.G. took one look at her and smiled. "You got the promotion, didn't you?"

Tina nodded.

"I knew you would. Congratulations, honey. Oh, this is so exciting."

She held out her arms. Tina leaned down and hugged her, blinking back sudden tears she didn't completely understand.

"Heavens, Tina. What in the world?"

"I didn't think I'd get the job," she said. Which didn't really explain the tears, but sounded plausible.

"Well, I did." G.G. gestured at a chair and Tina sat down. "Now, I want details."

"Well, my new job starts Monday. I'll be parceling out some of my work to others." Kendra, for one, and Tina did not look forward to that. She felt for the woman, who was sure to be sorely disappointed. "Oh, Jim says hello and Happy Thanksgiving."

"Isn't that sweet. My goodness, this is marvelous news. Tina Morrell, creative director. I love the sound of that." G.G. rubbed her hands together. "It won't be long until you're running the whole company."

Tina bit her lip. "If you're still this sick on Sunday... Well, we may need to bring in a nurse." Guilt-ridden, she hung her head. Caring for G.G. was *her* responsibility. "I know you don't want that, but..."

"For your career, I'll deal with it," G.G. said. "I wonder if my insurance will cover the costs."

That she gave in so easily only highlighted how important Tina's promotion was to her. "If you let me pay for it, I'll feel less guilty."

"I wouldn't want that. Let's check to see what the insurance covers."

"Okay, but I'll fill in any gaps. All right? I'll get on that right away, but it *is* the night before Thanksgiving, and I may not get answers until Friday." She'd call G.G.'s insurance agent on the way to see Dr. Lomax Friday morning. Tina hoped the doctor worked a miracle.

"Shall we announce your promotion at dinner tomorrow? Or do you want to tell people now?"

Tina thought about how happy Kate, Jefferson and G.G.'s neighbors would be. Then she thought about Ryan and Maggie. For some reason, she dreaded telling them, though she couldn't have said why. After all, Ryan had assured her more than once that she'd get this promotion.

This news was too important to share over the phone, but she didn't dare stop by his house tonight. Especially now, when Maggie was in bed.

All too vividly she remembered what had happened the last time she and Ryan had been alone there. With her strong feelings for him, that was too dangerous.

She'd tell him when he came here for Thanksgiving dinner tomorrow, she decided. That seemed far safer.

"I'll let Kate know now," she said. "Everyone else can wait."

Chapter Ten

Just before three o'clock on Thanksgiving Day, balancing a sweet potato casserole in one hand and holding on to Maggie with the other, Ryan headed out his door. In previous years, he and Maggie had shared the feast with friends in L.A.—usually at a restaurant. This would be his daughter's first Thanksgiving in someone's home, and she was impatient to get there. Ryan looked forward to a home-cooked meal with friends.

With Tina. It had only been two days since the kindergarten field trip. Yet knowing that in a few minutes he'd be with her… He was every bit as eager as Maggie.

Way too hot-blooded. He frowned.

"Daddy, come on." Maggie tugged his hand, and Ryan realized he'd come to a stop in his own front yard.

Today was for family and friends, not wayward desire. Equally important, this was a chance to reinforce the message that Tina would leave on Sunday. Once she left the island, he knew he'd be able to forget her. He only hoped Maggie would, too.

This afternoon he would enjoy himself. No lusting after Tina, and no worries about his job. Yet as his daughter pulled him forward, he couldn't help recalling his recent conversation with Bernard Beale.

"I have a great team and they're doing a damned good job," he'd told Beale when he'd finally reached him on the phone. "What they need now is some recognition for their achievements. If you'd send out a more positive e-mail I'd appreciate it."

"You'll hear from me on Monday," Beale had replied.

Whatever the hell that meant.

As soon as he and Maggie crossed the street, Ryan let go of her hand. She skipped up G.G.'s walkway, hopped onto the front stoop and rang the doorbell.

An instant later Tina opened it, wearing an apron and a pretty blue dress.

"Happy Thanksgiving, Tina!" Maggie bubbled. "Look, Daddy let me wear my princess dress again!"

"Let you?" Ryan rolled his eyes. "You refused to wear anything else."

Tina laughed. "Well, I happen to love that dress. You look beautiful, sweetie."

So did Tina. The rich color of her outfit made her eyes look as blue as a spring sky. Ryan's heart gave a joyous kick, and he realized that standing here looking at her he was way too happy.

He held out the casserole. "This needs to be reheated in the microwave."

"No problem," she said with a sideways look that he couldn't decipher. "Please, come in."

His daughter bounced through the door. "Where's G.G.?"

"In bed in the den," Tina said. "Jefferson's there, too, and they're waiting for you."

"Goody!" Maggie raced off.

Ryan stepped inside and closed the door. Delicious

aromas filled the air, making his mouth water. "Smells great in here. So G.G.'s really in bed?"

"I'm afraid so," Tina murmured, casting a worried look toward the den. "She's in way too much pain to sit at the table."

"I don't like the sound of this. If she's that sick we should leave, and you should call Dr. Dove right away. Even if it is Thanksgiving."

"I know. I even picked up the phone once." Tina gave a helpless shrug. "G.G. actually *yelled* at me, Ryan." She cringed. "So I hung up. She's always been so rational, but she sure isn't now."

"That's weird," he said. "At least she has that doctor's appointment in Anacortes tomorrow." He had to know. "If she's still this bad off on Sunday, will you be staying longer?"

"Well…" Her fingers fidgeted with the glass top of Ryan's casserole. "Um, the turkey will be ready soon, and I should microwave this. Could you come into the kitchen? We'll talk there."

Curious, he followed her past the dining room table, which was set for four. He'd never seen Tina in a dress before. She had slender, shapely legs. Nice.

"If G.G.'s eating in bed, we should eat with her in there," he suggested.

"That's a great idea—if she'll let us. There isn't much space, but I suppose we can fit our chairs around the bed." Tina set his casserole inside the microwave and programmed the time. "We'll have to eat from our laps, though. Will you carve the turkey when it's ready?"

"Sure." Ryan couldn't picture Maggie eating off her lap, but they'd work it out. He eyed Tina. "So, talk."

"There's something you should know." She frowned at

a spot on her apron, instead of looking at him. "G.G. wants me to announce this at dinner, so pretend you're surprised. Last night I found out that I got the promotion."

All along, he'd figured she would. Yet for some reason hearing it from her lips was like a sucker punch to his gut. "What'd I tell you?" he said, mustering a smile. "Congratulations."

"Thanks."

Tina didn't look as pleased as Ryan had expected her to. She was worried about G.G., he figured. "When do you start?"

"Monday. Before I forget, I'm done with your fax machine. Thanks for letting me borrow it. I set it on the bottom step for you. You asked whether I'm staying longer…" She let out a heavy sigh. "I've hired a nurse to take care of G.G., and I'm leaving Sunday afternoon."

Ryan knew she needed to go back to work, but with G.G. so sick and not getting better… This only reinforced how important Tina's career was to her. No big surprise.

Since he could think of nothing to say to that, he simply nodded and then turned away. "I'd best say hello to G.G. now."

HALF AN HOUR LATER, seated in a chair near G.G.'s bed, with a steaming plate on her lap, Tina thought the dear woman looked worse than ever. As gentle as Ryan and Jefferson had been when they'd propped her up in bed, she'd groaned in agony. Tina was too worried to eat. G.G. picked at her meal, which Tina had arranged on a bed tray, and tried to put on a cheerful face. But discomfort shadowed her eyes and bracketed her mouth, and everyone was subdued.

Even Maggie, who knelt in front of her chair and used

the seat as a table. Every few minutes she jumped up to hover behind Tina or kiss G.G.'s cheek.

Such a thoughtful, loving child, Tina thought, already wistful. She was really going to miss her. She'd miss Ryan just as much. And maybe after the guests left tonight, she'd call Dr. Dove whether G.G. wanted her to or not.

"We haven't shared our thanks," G.G. said, clinking her knife against her wineglass, which contained sparkling cider.

"Every Thanksgiving, we all share one thing we're thankful for. I'll start, and Tina, you go last."

Knowing G.G. expected her to give thanks for her promotion and announce it that way, Tina nodded.

"This year," G.G. went on, "I'm especially thankful for Ryan and Maggie." She glanced from one to the other. "The day you moved in was a lucky day, indeed."

Maggie beamed.

"Ditto," Ryan said, ducking his head. He was actually blushing! "Maggie and I are darned lucky we moved here. I'm thankful for your kindness to us, and for your warm welcome. This is such a special neighborhood, and we're glad to make our home here."

Though he didn't look at Tina, she sensed that he was talking to her. She wasn't certain she understood his message, though.

"Your turn, Maggie," G.G. said. "What are you thankful for?"

"I'm thankful for my teacher, and for Sam and Gina, Mr. Jeffries, and you and Tina."

She smiled at Tina, and Tina felt both blessed and sad. Sometimes she wished she'd stayed on the island, instead of going to college and grad school. Then, maybe…

Looking fiercely protective, Ryan cupped his daughter's shoulder, reminding Tina that he didn't want a relationship except with Maggie. Which, since she had a career to advance, was for the best.

"And I'm thankful that after Thanksgiving comes Christmas. Santa will come and bring me presents. Yippee!"

Everyone smiled.

"I'm up," Jefferson said. In honor of the day, he'd worn a coat and tie. "I'm thankful that Tina can cook almost as good as you, G.G."

Despite her pain, G.G. managed a chuckle, and Tina and Ryan both smiled, grateful for the momentary lightening of their concern for G.G.

"And I'm grateful to be sharing this meal with you," Jefferson finished.

"Now you, Tina," G.G. said with an expectant look.

For a split second Ryan's gaze connected with Tina's. She wished she knew what he was thinking, but his expression was unreadable.

"I'm grateful to announce that I got the promotion we all hoped for," she said.

G.G. couldn't have looked more pleased. "Isn't that wonderful?"

"I knew you'd get it." Jefferson whistled through his fingers, then applauded.

Maggie clapped, too, even though she probably didn't understand.

Ryan already had congratulated her. Now he did so again, with a stiff nod.

"What's a 'romotion?" Maggie asked.

"Promotion," Ryan corrected. "What it means is Tina got that job she wanted."

Maggie's forehead wrinkled, so Tina explained. "Remember when I flew to Seattle and back on that noisy seaplane?"

The little girl nodded.

"I did that to interview for a better job."

This time Ryan's face was easier to read. He was concerned for his child. "Tina's new job starts on Monday and she's leaving Sunday," he told Maggie. "That's in three days."

"Three days? But that's really soon."

Maggie's stricken look wrenched Tina's heart. "I've been telling you all along that I would have to leave," she said. "But I promise I'll be back for Christmas. That's only a few weeks from now."

"Try to be happy for her, Maggie," G.G. said. "I am, and I'm so proud of you, Tina."

But she wouldn't be if she knew how Tina really felt—that when she drove away from Huckleberry Hill Road and caught the ferry for home, she'd be leaving part of her heart on Halo Island.

HOURS AFTER leaving G.G.'s, sitting in his own kitchen, Ryan nursed a beer and thought about the day. The Thanksgiving dinner that he'd looked forward to hadn't turned out at all the way he'd expected. Damn, but he wished things were different. For starters, he wished that Maggie understood why Tina was leaving. Because no matter what she'd said before, she didn't get it at all. In her five-year-old mind Tina was leaving the island—and her—because somehow she'd done something to drive her away. Which was ridiculous. At his wit's end, Ryan had tried to explain that she had nothing to do with Tina's leaving. He did it several times in different ways, but still his daughter was inconsolable.

He swore in desperation. And decided that first thing in the morning he'd call Dr. Dove and ask for the name of a competent family therapist. Tonight, feeling helpless and scared for Maggie, he'd read her two funny stories and had stayed in her room longer than usual, until she finally drifted off.

No doubt to suffer through a night of bad dreams. Ryan raked his hands through his hair. Again he'd failed to protect his child. For that, he figured he'd have a few nightmares of his own.

And he'd miss Tina, too. He laughed out loud, a harsh sound that caused him to wince, and tried to ignore the empty feeling in his chest.

How had she gotten under his skin so quickly? Ryan couldn't explain it, but he knew she had, and he'd pay for that. Big-time.

The ringing phone broke through his thoughts. Frowning, he pushed himself to his feet, moved to the counter and eyed his caller ID. *Georgia Garwood.*

Since it was after eleven, Ryan figured it was Tina. She'd never called before, and wouldn't unless something was wrong. He snatched the phone from its cradle. "Tina. What's happened to G.G.?"

"You saw her this afternoon. The pain is even worse now. Excruciating. She has a fever, too." She paused, and he pictured her chewing her lower lip. "Something's very wrong."

Ryan hid his alarm. "Did you call Dr. Dove?"

"Yes, and we're supposed to meet him at the clinic right away. But I can't get G.G. out of bed, and once I do, I don't know how I'll get her into the car. I could call for an ambulance, but—"

"Forget the ambulance." Ryan headed for the coat closet to grab his jacket. "Give me five minutes to get Norma over here to stay with Maggie, and I'll be there."

Chapter Eleven

At eleven forty-five Thanksgiving night, the waiting room of the Halo Island Clinic was silent and empty. Sharing the beige vinyl sofa with Ryan wasn't necessary. Or wise. But when he'd sat down close beside Tina, his shoulder, arm and thigh warm and solid against hers, she hadn't objected. She welcomed his wordless empathy and support. At the moment she didn't much care that she shouldn't be with him. She needed him close by, and that was all that mattered. That and G.G. Tina prayed she would be all right.

As the second hand on the wall clock silently ticked off the minutes, she clasped her hands together tightly in her lap.

"Sitting here, not knowing anything is killing me. I wish to goodness G.G. had let me stay in the examining room with her."

"She's always struck me as an independent spirit," Ryan said.

"I know, but this could be life-threatening. If anything happens to her…" The thought was too horrible to bear, and though the room was warm, Tina shivered.

Ryan settled his arm around her shoulders and drew her closer—a great comfort.

"She'll be okay, Tina. I know it."

"I hope you're right." Hardly aware of her actions, Tina nestled against his side, resting her head on his shoulder. "I just wish I'd forced her into the clinic yesterday or even this morning."

"You tried, remember? Stubborn woman refused to go. Dr. Dove said to bring her in if she had a fever. That's exactly what you did."

"I know, but still…I should've realized how sick she was. You pointed that out, but I didn't listen." Instead, she'd been so wrapped up in herself, thinking about her work and about how sad she'd feel to leave Ryan and Maggie, that she'd all but ignored G.G. Filled with remorse, she buried her face in her hands. "I feel so guilty."

"Hey." Ryan tipped up her chin. His eyes beamed warmth into her. "Like you told me the other night, don't be so hard on yourself. She's in good hands now. Dr. Dove will take care of her."

With all her heart, Tina hoped he was right.

They sat without speaking further for what seemed forever, Tina absorbing Ryan's strength.

When Dr. Dove finally emerged from the examining room, she ducked out from under Ryan's arm. Not before the doctor's gray eyebrows raised a fraction, though. So he'd noticed her and Ryan, all warm and cozy. She hoped he wouldn't mention this to his wife, who, though a kind and thoughtful woman, was more than likely to spread the word.

Tina stood up and hurried forward. "How is she?" She didn't see G.G. "Where is she?"

"She's resting on the examining table."

Why had he left her there? Tina started toward the inner room, but Dr. Dove touched her arm, stopping her. "She's comfortable enough for now, and we need to talk."

Heart pounding with fear, Tina nodded.

Suddenly, Ryan was at her side. "Please go ahead," he said.

The doctor's shrewd gaze flitted from him to Tina. "It's okay if Ryan hears this," she assured him.

Dr. Dove stroked the bald spot on top of his head and nodded. "She has a staph infection, probably from the surgery."

"Dear God." Beyond caring what Dr. Dove thought, Tina reached for Ryan's hand. His fingers curled around hers.

"We caught it in time. It's serious, but at the moment, it's not life-threatening."

"At the moment?" she asked, numb with terror.

"She should be fine."

Tina clung to the certainty in Dr. Dove's voice. "Thank goodness," she whispered, sinking against Ryan in relief. Seconds later, confused, she frowned. "But it's been weeks since the operation. I don't understand why she'd get an infection now."

"It's rare, but there have been cases where an infection sets in years after surgery. Now, I've consulted Dr. Lomax, the doctor in Anacortes who was supposed to see her tomorrow. We're in agreement that Georgia should start on antibiotics immediately. I've given her a shot, but she needs professional care. We want her to check into the hospital in Anacortes tonight."

"Tonight?" Tina massaged the place between her eyebrows, where a headache had bloomed. "But it's Thanksgiving, and the ferries don't run this late. How am I supposed to get her there?"

"The medical boat is standing by, and an ambulance is on the way to take her to the dock."

This was good news. "All right. I'm going with her."

"I already notified the medical staff that you would," Dr. Dove said.

Flashing lights outside the window alerted them that the ambulance had arrived. The paramedics strode in with a stretcher, and for a while the clinic bustled with activity.

While two muscular men brought G.G. out on the stretcher and consulted with Dr. Dove, Tina turned to Ryan. "Thank you so much, Ryan. I don't know how I'd have made it tonight without you."

"I'm not leaving now," he said. "I'll drive down to the dock and meet you there."

He'd already gone beyond what a good neighbor would do. He was as special as G.G. had said and more, and Tina was closer than ever to falling in love with him. She shook her head. "You should get home to Maggie."

"She's asleep. If she wakes up, Norma will explain." Ryan shrugged and looked at her.

"What about work? Don't you have to go in tomorrow?"

"I'll let Jason know I'll be in late."

Tina could think of no other reasons for him to stay on the island. Besides, she wanted him to come with her.

The paramedics were ready to leave, and G.G. beckoned her over. "I feel so silly about this," she said, looking sheepish. "Don't you dare let this stop you from going home Sunday."

That G.G. was thinking about her career at a time like this... Well, it only reinforced how important Tina's success was to her. Tina sensed that Ryan was watching and listening. She glanced at him. His concerned expression had faded, and his face was now carefully blank.

Her eyes filled up. Not wanting G.G. to know how anxious and upset she was, she hastily blinked away the tears and forced a smile. "Don't you worry about anything but getting well," she said, brushing stray strands of hair from the older woman's forehead.

"Of course I'm worried. I don't want anything to get in the way of your new job."

"Ready to go?"

Tina followed the paramedics to the waiting ambulance.

WEARY CLEAR to his bones, Ryan followed the ambulance to the dock. Tina had all but told him to go home. He could make a U-turn and head for Huckleberry Hill Road without a shred of guilt. Instead, he continued toward the water.

Thing was, Tina needed him. He admired her tough don't-worry-about-me-I'm-fine act with G.G., but he knew she was close to falling apart. The way she'd sunk against his side on the couch. Reaching for his hand and holding tight when Dr. Dove delivered his news—she needed a shoulder to lean on. His.

Ryan liked that way more than he should, and was glad she'd called him tonight. He didn't stop to wonder why that made him feel so good; he knew only that he wasn't going to leave her now.

He detested hospitals and hadn't been in one since Heidi's death three and a half years earlier. But he figured Tina would appreciate his company tonight. He would go to Anacortes with her and G.G., provided Norma agreed to stay the night. She'd be well paid for this, and Ryan would thank her husband, Harry. Maybe he'd treat the man to a game of golf in the spring. Hadn't Tina suggested he make some friends?

Slipping his cell phone from his jacket pocket, he phoned Norma. "G.G.'s going to the hospital in Anacortes tonight," he said. "On the medical boat."

"Then it's serious." She sounded worried.

"Maybe, or maybe not."

Ryan explained everything while keeping an eye on the road. "Can you stay tonight? You're welcome to use my bed."

"I'll sleep on the couch," she said.

"Listen, Maggie will probably have nightmares."

He told Norma what to do—give her a glass of water, a sympathetic ear and plenty of reassurance.

"No problem," Norma said. "I'll consider it training for my future child's bad dreams."

Ryan hoped to hell that her kid grew up feeling safe and loved and escaped such miserable stuff.

"Please send G.G. my love and wishes for a speedy recovery," Norma said.

"Will do."

He was almost at the dock now. His thoughts returned to Tina. He'd offer whatever she needed to make it through the night. Anything she wanted from him, he'd give. *Anything.*

Possibilities filled his head, all of them hot and sexual. Damned if his body didn't stir to life. Ryan muttered and gripped the steering wheel tighter. G.G. was headed for the hospital, and Tina was worried sick. What kind of self-absorbed man was he, thinking about sex right now?

What Tina needed was a friend. He could be that. Even Maggie understood about friends. The thought eased his mind, and he began to relax.

A SOFT HAND shook Ryan awake. He opened his eyes to find Tina standing in front of him. He'd been dozing in a waiting room chair while the nurses attended to G.G. Thanks to Tina, she had a private room.

"How's she doing?" he asked.

"Not great." Weariness blunted Tina's features and showed in her voice. "She wants to talk to you."

"Me?" He sat up and rubbed a hand over his face, absently noting that he needed a shave. "What does she want?"

"Heck if I know, but she's exhausted and so am I, and the nurses want us gone, so make it quick. She's in the last room on the right."

Leaving Tina glassy-eyed in the deserted waiting room, Ryan strode down the tiled hallway. Most of the rooms were dark, but in some of them machines beeped and flashed. Antiseptic smells assaulted him, reminding him of that time with Heidi, and he flinched.

Wearing a hospital gown, G.G. lay covered to her armpits with white blankets. In the harsh fluorescent lights, she looked ashen and exhausted. The bed was propped up at a twenty-degree angle, and an IV was attached to the back of one hand. Nearby, a monitor displayed numbers that Ryan couldn't decipher.

She didn't look as if she wanted company, and Ryan hesitated in the doorway. "You asked to see me?"

"Hello, Ryan." With a weak wave of her free hand she gestured him forward.

He pulled over an orange chair and sat down beside her, close to her head. "How you doing, G.G.?"

"I think I'll live."

"You're too feisty not to." The alternative was too painful to contemplate.

As sick as she was, she managed a smile. "I'm not letting those hospital people keep me here long."

"That's what I like to hear."

She clasped his hand in a surprisingly firm grip, and he bent toward her. "Though I've only known you and Maggie a few months, you've become as dear to me as my own flesh and blood. I don't know what Tina and I would've done tonight without you. Thank you."

The heartfelt words touched him. His vision blurred and he swallowed thickly. "I meant what I said at dinner this afternoon," he returned, in a gruff voice. "You've been so kind to Maggie and me. This is the least I can do."

She tugged him closer and lowered her voice to a whisper. "Tina acts like she's strong and tough, but I know her. I'm all she has, and she's scared. Promise me you'll keep an eye on her tonight."

As one who understood only too well the fear of loss, Ryan was happy to do this. "You have my word."

A nurse bustled in, a stern look on her face. "Miss Garwood needs her rest. Visiting hours start at nine in the morning."

He let go of G.G.'s hand, slid back the chair and stood. "Should I send Tina back in?"

"No," G.G. said. "I'm tired, and we've said our good-nights. Don't forget your promise, Ryan."

He nodded. "Try to get some rest."

Tina hadn't moved since he'd left her. She was still in the chair he'd vacated, eyes closed and head against the wall. Ryan hated to wake her, but if he didn't her neck was sure to hurt. She needed a bed.

He hunkered down beside her and touched her arm. Her eyes flickered open, instantly focused. "Did you see G.G.?"

"Yeah, but she and the nurses ordered me out. Why don't we find a motel around here and get some rest."

"I can't leave. What if something goes wrong?"

"G.G.'s in good hands here. She needs you strong and rested. The hospital has your cell number. If anyone needs to reach you, they'll call." He stood, then offered her a hand up.

"All right." With a weary sigh she let him pull her to her feet.

Grasping her arm, Ryan headed for the nurse's station, where two nurses kept a watchful eye on things.

"Is there a motel around here?" he asked.

"Closest one is a block away," the younger nurse replied. She gave directions, and Ryan and Tina headed for the elevators.

In weary silence they left the hospital and headed out through fog and bone-chilling dampness.

The motel, which was part of a chain, looked like any other motel, with gray and mauve furniture, a large bouquet of fake flowers on a low table and an eating area off to one side.

The heavyset middle-aged male clerk's badge identified him as Fred. Squinting, he checked the computer screen, his shirt stretched tight over his belly. "We don't have any rooms with king-size beds available. You folks mind a queen-size?"

He thought Ryan and Tina were together.

Tina flushed. "Um, we need separate rooms."

Fred's gaping jaw and arched eyebrows were almost comical. "Oh. Sure. Connecting all right? For your *protection*," he winked, "both doors have inside locks."

"Thanks." Ryan ignored the sly wink. Let the man think what he wanted, but both doors would stay locked. He thought about his promise to G.G., certain she hadn't meant for him to spend the night with Tina. This way he'd be close by, available should she need him.

"We had a medical emergency and didn't have time to pack. Do you have travel kits?" he asked.

Reaching under the counter, Fred pulled out two plastic packets containing toothpaste, toothbrush, comb and plastic razor. "I hope the person will be okay."

Tina closed her eyes a moment, then opened them. "Thank you."

They scheduled wake-up calls for eight-thirty, then silently rode the elevator to the third floor, Tina swallowing rapidly as if working to hold back her emotions. Ryan guessed that she was trying not to cry in front of him. At the moment, giving her the privacy she clearly needed was impossible, so he shoved the packet and his hands in his jeans' pocket and stared at the carpet.

Their rooms were several yards from the elevator. As they stopped before Tina's door, her lower lip trembled. "Thank you again, Ryan." Her eyes flooded. "For being here. You've been wonderful."

God help him, the dam burst and she began to sob. He opened his arms, and she fell into them.

He'd never been any good with crying women, but he knew what worked with Maggie. He patted Tina's back and murmured whatever came into his head. "It's okay, Tina. G.G.'s getting the best care possible. She's a fighter, and she'll be fine."

"I kn-know, but I'm scared anyway," she said, her words muffled by his shirt.

After a while she pulled away, sniffled and found a packet of tissues in her purse. "I don't know why I'm crying. And on your only shirt." Using a clean tissue she swiped at his wet shirtfront. "I'm sorry."

"Don't worry about it." He put his arm around her waist. "You're exhausted. Give me your key."

Holding her close, he opened the door and shepherded her inside. The small room smelled faintly of disinfectant. He turned back the ugly brown-and-red-striped spread. "Get some rest, and I'll see you tomorrow."

Tina gave him a weak smile. "G.G. said you were a special man. Now I know why."

Ryan felt his cheeks grow warm. "I'm just a regular guy

who happens to care a lot about the woman who lives across the street."

And the woman standing in front of him, too. He wished to God he didn't, but there it was.

"Modest, too." This time her smile was stronger.

She cupped his cheek, her hand soft and warm. Feelings he didn't want or understand crowded his chest, and against his better judgment he closed his eyes and savored her touch. When he opened them her gaze was dark and probing.

What he saw there—need and hunger—fanned the fires he'd battled for days. His body woke up, and he knew that if he stayed any longer he wouldn't be able to leave.

Clearing his throat he pulled away. "Good night." He strode toward the door.

Just before he walked through it, aiming his gaze at a point above her shoulder so that he wouldn't see the desire in her face, he spoke again. "If you need anything, you know where to find me." With his door locked and his mind blank—he would not think about wanting Tina. "Knock if you need me."

Hoping to hell she wouldn't, he headed for his room. Seconds later, he heard water sluicing through the pipes— probably her shower. He showered, too, another cold one, then washed out his socks and his shorts. Though feeling as he did, sleeping in the buff would only make things worse.

Glancing down at his semihard arousal, he shook his head. Things were pretty bad now.

He folded back his striped bedspread. The soft mattress dipped under his weight. He'd probably wake up with a mother of a backache, but was too tired to let that bother him.

As he lay in the darkness, he tried not to think about Tina. Only a thin wall and two locked doors separated them. Was she naked, too, or sleeping in her underwear? Ryan wondered whether she wore the plain cotton kind or something sexier. Lacy, he decided, picturing her in slinky panties and a low-cut bra that barely hid her assets. His arousal stiffened. He groaned. It served him right.

Chapter Twelve

Wrapped in a bath towel, her freshly washed underwear and socks hanging in the bathroom to dry, Tina rubbed a clear space on the steamed-up mirror and pulled a comb through her hair. Come morning, without hair gel, she'd never be able to fix it the way she liked. The bathroom had no hairdryer, and she was too exhausted to call and ask for one.

She looked as tired as she felt, and small wonder. What a night this had been. And it wasn't over. Despite knowing rationally that G.G. would pull through, Tina's heart stuttered with terror at the thought that she might not. Tears filled her eyes again, blurring her reflection.

She turned away, grabbed a tissue, blew her nose and admitted that she didn't want to be alone tonight.

No, she wanted to sleep in Ryan's bed, and forget for a little while about G.G., her new job as creative director, and how mixed up she was. In Ryan's arms, she knew she would find the solace she sought.

What about your heart? the logical part of her brain asked. If she made love with Ryan… That was a surefire way to lose her heart to him. Which he didn't want. Really, neither did she. Not with her new position to focus on.

"None of that matters tonight," she stated out loud. At the moment that was true. "I need him."

Just for this one night, away from the island, where no one besides her and Ryan would ever know.

New doubts plagued her. *What if he rejects me?* With circles under her puffy, red-rimmed eyes, no makeup and wet hair, she was hardly attractive. But she wasn't blind. She'd seen the desire in his eyes; had felt it in his embrace. His hunger was every bit as strong as hers.

"Knock, if you need me," he'd said.

And she did, desperately. Before she changed her mind, feeling bold and a little reckless, she marched toward the door that separated their rooms.

RYAN WAS seriously considering taking care of his arousal problem all by himself, when a firm knock on the door between his room and Tina's stopped him.

"Ryan?" Tina said, sounding dangerously close.

Swearing under his breath, he sat up and flipped on the light, blinking as his eyes adjusted to the brightness. "Yeah?"

"Would you please unlock your door?"

"What for?" he asked, wary and on edge.

"So I can come in. Please."

The need and anguish in her voice were impossible to ignore. "I'm not dressed," he warned, hoping to hell his body settled down.

"That's okay. I'm not, either."

Not what he wanted to hear. Images filled his head, of Tina naked. Heart pounding, he stepped into his jeans and tried to zip them up. Given his present condition, this was not easy and not fun. Maybe Tina wouldn't notice. *Right, and life is full of happy endings.* He flipped the lock and opened the door a scant inch.

She was standing there with a skimpy white towel wrapped around her like a sarong, revealing pale bare shoulders and lots of leg, her face clean and her hair wet and freshly combed.

He'd never seen a more beautiful woman, and he yearned to pull off that towel and feast his eyes and hands on her. A certain part of his body throbbed. Blood hammered in his head, and he gripped the door between them.

"What is it?" he asked, his voice sounding brusque even to him.

"I don't want to be alone tonight." Her gaze never wavering from his, she drew a deep breath. "Can I stay with you?"

A bad idea, and they both knew it. Yet Ryan could no more turn her down than stop breathing. He stepped back and fully opened the door.

RYAN HAD LIED. He *was* dressed, partially, and every bit as gorgeous without his shirt as Tina had imagined. She ran her gaze over his muscled arms, the smattering of dark hair on his broad chest and his flat belly. Her eyes lowered to his strained zipper. He was aroused. Heat scalded her face, and abruptly she shifted her gaze.

"You see that I want you." His eyes glittered and a pained smile flickered. "Now, if you know what's good for you, you'll head back to your room and lock your door. And for God's sake, put on some clothes."

Standing stiff and tall, his expression harsh, he seemed almost ferocious. But Tina refused to be intimidated. Having left her pride behind, she wasn't about to back down.

She held her head high. "What's best for me tonight is staying here with you. I want to make love with you."

A strangled sound escaped from his throat. "Don't tempt me, Tina." Shaking his head, he backed away. "I can't get involved. I won't."

"I'm not asking for promises or commitment. All I want is tonight." She hated begging—she'd never done so before. And though she might hate herself in the morning, her feelings tonight pushed her beyond caring. "Help me forget about G.G. for a while." Hiding nothing from him, she reached out. "I need you, Ryan."

TINA'S EYES were hot and seeking, her tempting lower lip was there for the taking. And her arms, reaching for him as if she had a window into his fantasies and wanted to fulfill them…

Ryan's body throbbed mercilessly for release and his thoughts grew clouded. With the woman of his hottest dreams standing half-naked in front of him, how could he think straight? He couldn't think at all.

But he damn well should—for both their sakes. "Are you sure about this?"

Tina opened the towel and let it drop. "Does that answer your question?"

Now she was completely naked. Like a man dying of thirst, Ryan drank in the sight of her body, and his control disappeared. The round breasts and proud, dusky peaks seemed to beg him to touch and taste. The soft swell of her hips and the light brown thatch at the apex of her thighs. Dear God.

His throat tightened with emotion and his mouth went dry. He nodded. "You're beautiful. I wish I could make love with you, but I don't have protection with me." A partial solution occurred to him, however, and he raised his eyebrows. "I could still pleasure you, though."

"We don't need protection. I'm on the pill. I have been

since the age of fifteen, to regulate my cycle. It's been a while since I've been with a man, and I'm sure that I'm clean."

Two problems solved. He nodded. "I'm healthy, too."

As badly as he wanted to make love with her, he still wasn't convinced he should. "If we do this, it can only happen tonight." He wanted to cradle her face in his hands and study her eyes, but he didn't. Because once he touched her, there would be no turning back. "When we're back on the island…"

"It'll be as if nothing happened," she said. "I understand, and that's okay with me."

Tina did not flinch from his level look, and Ryan believed her. They were on the same page. Which was a relief, since he didn't think he could step away from her. Not now.

He moved closer, the desire in her expression tethering him as surely as a rope.

Her brows arched. "So we're—"

Too hungry to wait for her to finish whatever she meant to say, he captured her mouth. Warm and yielding, she tasted even better than he remembered.

Standing on her toes, she twined her hands around his neck. Her soft breasts pillowed against his chest, causing the sweetest kind of torture. Wanting her closer, he lifted her up and wrapped her thighs around his waist. He felt the dampness between her legs. *Wet.* For him.

Sweet mercy, he wanted her. Wanted to pleasure her all night long, and give her what she needed—blissful release from her troubles. Gripping her round, soft behind, devouring her mouth with his, he moved haltingly toward the bed.

He settled her on the sheets, her head on his pillow. Her eyes searched his, the heat and longing there arousing him as surely as a touch.

Leaving the lamp on so that he could watch her passion, he darted his tongue across her nipples. They drew tight and swelled with arousal. He nipped lightly and her breathing turned shallow and her head moved restlessly.

Ryan suckled her, enjoying the small sounds of pleasure that issued from her throat.

"Like that, do you?" he murmured.

In answer, she arched toward him. "Do it some more."

So he did, losing himself in her womanly scent and her shuddering breaths. As he pleasured her breasts, he skimmed his hand down her smooth stomach and past her thatch. She opened her thighs. *Yes.* He teased the sensitive bud between her legs. Moaning, she raised her hips.

Pleasing her this way was almost as good as burying himself in her, and Ryan, too, moaned. With two fingers, he entered her wet channel. She was hot and so fine.

When he sensed she was near climax, he watched her face. Arousal flushed her skin, and both nipples glistened from his attention. His own need was so intense, he wanted to take her hard and fast. But this was about her.

"I want to taste more of you," he said.

Alert to every tremble and hitch of her breath, he knelt between her legs. Her erotic, womanly scent filled his senses. He kissed the tender skin on her inner thighs, moving closer and closer to that sweet nub. She was pleading now, lifting her lips in supplication.

Parting her folds, he licked her sex.

"Finally." She sighed and tangled her hands in his hair while he teased and tasted her thoroughly. Suddenly, she pushed him away. "Ryan, I'm about to lose it."

"Go ahead, honey. Let go."

An instant later, she convulsed around his fingers.

Though his own body pulsed and ached for release, satisfaction rolled through him. He kissed the underside of her breast, just below her heart, then pulled her close to his side. "Feel better?"

"Mmm, yes." She raised her head and smiled at him with lips red and slightly swollen from his kisses. "But what about you?"

"This isn't about me," he said.

"Oh, no?"

Her fingers worked at his zipper and tortured his groin. And he was lost.

RYAN'S HEAVY-LIDDED EYES smoldered, as if he wanted to devour Tina. Sated a few seconds earlier, she suddenly wanted more. She wanted Ryan inside her. Her hands shook as she tugged his zipper.

He made a rasping sound and pushed her away. "I'll do it." Standing, he kicked off his jeans, and at last he was naked. His erection was glorious.

Mine. "You're huge."

"For you." He stood still, watching her with undisguised hunger, and letting her look her fill.

Unable to bear another instant without touching him, she patted the bed. "Come and lie down."

She licked her lips, and smiled to herself when his light brown eyes darkened to chocolate.

When he joined her, she pushed him onto his back. Feeling deliciously powerful, she kissed him, tasting herself on his mouth. Licked and nipped his nipples as he had hers, and slowly kissed her way down his belly. As she moved toward his groin, he tensed and sucked in a breath.

Tina closed her mouth over the velvety head of his shaft. A growl rose from his chest. Cupping the back of her head, he urged her closer. She pleasured him for all of one heartbeat.

Then, abruptly, she was on her back, with Ryan poised between her legs, his intense gaze burning into her.

"Are you ready?"

In answer, she scissored her legs around his waist, bringing her center flush with his arousal.

He slid in slowly, hesitating, giving her time to adjust to his length and size. The pleasure was so exquisite, she thought she might die.

"You feel so good," he whispered, his breath hot in her ear. "I'm going to make this last a long time."

Gritting his teeth he began to move with excruciating slowness. Deep in, then out, pulling so far back he almost left her. Then a slow slide in again. Over and over, each time bringing her closer to the edge. She let out a frustrated groan.

"Tell me what you want," he said.

"More. Harder. Faster."

"Like this?" He drove so deep, he surely touched her very core.

"That's good," she breathed, her focus narrowing to the place where they joined. "Yes. Oh, yes."

He moved fast, exactly the way she wanted it, each stroke coiling her tighter, lifting her higher, until she soared.

Her climax was shattering, made all the more intense when Ryan called out her name and came with her. The world fell away and for long seconds there was only the two of them and more pleasure and joy than she'd ever imagined.

As she drifted back to earth, her head resting against his thudding heart, his strong arms holding her close, she was awash in tenderness and love. Yes, love. She loved Ryan, but he'd never know.

If her heart broke later—and it would—at least for this moment she was at peace.

"That was intense, amazing," he murmured, stroking her hip. "Did I take your mind off G.G.?"

That and all Tina's other worries. "You certainly did. You are a wonderful lover, Ryan Chase." She pressed her lips to his chest, so he wouldn't see the love in her eyes. "Thank you."

He kissed the top of her head. "It was my very great pleasure."

Safe and secure in Ryan's arms, at least for what was left of the night, Tina slept.

Chapter Thirteen

When Tina awoke she was on her side, facing the wall. Ryan's arm was slung over her shoulder, and his body was molded to her backside, spoon-style. Sharing his bed was heaven. She snuggled closer. Feeling his arousal against her, she smiled to herself. Even asleep, he wanted her. Well, she shared his hunger. They'd made love twice already during their few hours together. Now she wanted him again.

As she turned toward him, both motel phones rang— the one in her room and the one on Ryan's bedside table.

G.G. Tina forgot about making love. Suddenly anxious, she jerked away from Ryan and lunged for the phone.

"Nothing to worry about," he said in a deep, scratchy morning voice. "Those are our wake-up calls."

She lifted the receiver to find that he was right.

"If the hospital needed you, they'd call you on your cell," he said. "I haven't heard it ring. But then…" He grinned, a sexy, intimate smile that wreaked havoc on her. "I was kinda distracted."

He was sleep-tousled, with a crease on his cheek from the covers. Tina's heart filled with love. And gratitude.

Their brief night together had been beautiful. She hated

for it to end, hated to leave the oasis of their bed. But it was morning now, and time to return to reality. They would never make love again. Ryan would never know that she loved him and he would never love her. At least he was honest about that.

She only hoped that he hadn't guessed her feelings. But she was good at hiding how she felt—didn't G.G. and the others believe she loved her work? She would hide this, too.

"Time to get up," she said in a cheerful voice so false, it made her wince. Modestly, she wrapped the blanket around her and sat up.

"Hey." Ryan sat up, too. He cupped her face and looked into her eyes. "Are you okay?"

She saw warmth and concern, but not what she really wanted—love.

"A little tired." In an effort to lighten the mood, she elbowed him gently. "A certain big guy kept me busy last night, when I probably should've been sleeping."

Ryan's grin was full of male pride. "Guilty as charged."

"I should shower," she said, half hoping he would invite himself to join her.

"Me, too."

He rolled out of bed and tossed her the towel she'd worn the night before, and she knew he wasn't going to. It really was over.

She wrapped herself in the terry cloth and stood up.

"I'll meet you in the lobby in ten minutes," Ryan said, walking her to the door between their rooms.

Then she heard the lock click into place.

It's better this way, Tina told herself. With G.G. and her new job to worry about, now was not the right time to fall in love.

STANDING BENEATH the pounding hot water, Ryan imagined Tina with him. Washing each other, sharing hot kisses, making love under the spray.

His body sprang to life, and now he wanted her more than ever. He swore to himself, but he wasn't sorry about sharing his bed with her. What he regretted was the fact that they'd started something that could never go beyond one night.

The single saving grace was that Tina agreed. career-wise, she was fully committed and had no time for a relationship—was no different than it had been with the other women he'd gotten involved with and been hurt by.

Only this time he wasn't involved.

Uh-huh. He muttered a few more choice names at himself before stepping out of the shower.

His shorts were still damp, but they'd have to do. As soon as he shaved and dressed, he'd check in with Norma and say good-morning to Maggie. Then, he'd make that call to Jason. Later, after he stopped by the hospital and checked on G.G., he'd catch a ferry back to the island. He'd left his car in the parking lot at the ferry terminal, making it easy to get home, change and head for the bank.

Back on Halo Island, he meant to act as if last night had never happened. Not easy, but he'd handle it. And so would Tina.

"THE DOCTORS WANT G.G. to stay in the hospital at least one more night," Tina told Kate.

She was calling from the waiting room, while G.G. napped. At midmorning, the hospital was crowded with people and conversation buzzed around her. "If I'd waited one more day to bring her in, she'd have needed another surgery." An alarming prospect, for sure. Tina was profoundly grateful to Dr. Dove. And the paramedics who'd delivered G.G. safely to the hospital, Dr. Lomax and the knowledgeable nursing staff.

"What a relief that she doesn't need another operation," Kate said. "Have you lined up a nurse for when she comes home?"

"Yes, and I feel terrible about that."

"Well, you just stop right now. With your new job starting Monday, it can't be helped."

Which was true. Tina had promised Jim Sperling she'd be there, and G.G. insisted she follow through. Her stomach began to burn.

"I know," she said, digging through her purse for the antacids. "But I can't help wishing I could stay until she's well again."

On the other hand, with Ryan across the street, and both of them pretending nothing had happened last night... It was best if she left.

"So," Kate said, the mild singsong tone alerting Tina that she was about to utter some interesting tidbit. "I hear Ryan Chase went with you and G.G. to Anacortes. I *am* your best friend. Exactly when were you planning on telling me?"

Either Dr. Dove had talked, or Norma Featherstone, or maybe one of the paramedics. Tina should've known her best friend would find out.

"Um, I wanted to," she murmured into the cell, "only it's not exactly private around here." Though she didn't know a soul in the room, and no one seemed to be paying the slightest bit of attention to her.

"You're forgiven, but only if you tell me *everything*."

"Everything?" Tina wasn't sure about that. "Hang on a sec." To be on the safe side, she moved into a small alcove by the elevator.

"Ryan was amazing," she said quietly, as a middle-aged

couple approached, one of them pushing the elevator button. "He was a huge help and a comfort to both G.G. and me."

She remembered the terrifying wait in the Halo Island Clinic and thought about how she'd absorbed his strength while they waited for Dr. Dove to finish examining G.G. Without Ryan there, she'd have been a blubbering basket case. "So when he offered to ride with us in the ambulance boat…"

Kate made a sound of admiration. "That man has a heart of gold."

A heart that was off-limits to Tina. "That he does," she said with a sad smile. "He stayed until an hour ago, then left to catch the ferry back." With a quick hug and a kiss on the cheek, the coolness and control more painful than comforting. Tina couldn't stifle a heartfelt sigh.

"That sigh sounded awfully dreary. Lovesick, even. Something must've happened between you two."

Kate was entirely too perceptive. Since grade school they'd shared their deepest secrets—everything except Tina's recent ambivalence about her career. No one knew about that. But in matters of the heart, yes, and Tina knew she could trust Kate. Still, she hesitated.

"Listen, if you don't want to share, don't."

Good friend that Kate was, she didn't sound at all offended. Which inclined Tina, all the more, to confide in her.

"Of course I want to, Kate." Again, she lowered her voice. "Swear you'll keep this to yourself."

"I solemnly swear," Kate said. "If you could see me, you'd be watching me cross my heart right now."

"Okay." Tina blew out a breath. "I was so upset about G.G. last night," she said, "that when Ryan and I checked into the motel near the hospital, they gave us connecting rooms…"

She told her friend what she wanted to know. That she hadn't wanted to sleep alone and that, for Maggie's sake, Ryan didn't want a relationship. She left out nothing, not even the part where she'd begged him to make love to her. "He's a thoughtful, fantastic lover, and I've fallen in love with him," she finished.

"That's wonderful, Tina! It couldn't have happened to two finer people."

Though Kate couldn't see her, she made a face. "Did you not hear what I said? Ryan can't get involved. He's afraid Maggie will end up getting hurt. And anyway, I'll be leaving soon."

"Sounds to me as if he already *is* involved," Kate said. "As for the long-distance thing, that's why God invented transportation."

She made it all sound so easy. "Yes, but Ryan and I both agreed that last night was a one-time thing."

The elevator dinged and the doors opened. Tina turned her back on it, and tried to concentrate.

"Then you're both kidding yourselves," Kate said. "If you don't get together again, I'll eat my apron."

Tina snorted. "It's not that simple. If Ryan doesn't—"

"*There* she is," exclaimed a familiar female voice.

"Hello, Tina." This came from a crusty male voice she also recognized.

Tina pivoted to find Rose Thorne and Sidney Pletcher, both bearing gifts for G.G. They must have stepped off the elevator when her back was turned.

She waved, then signaled that she'd be a minute.

"Rose and Sidney are here, so I'd better go," she told Kate. "I'll call you back later."

"A SHAME YOU MISSED Ryan," G.G. told her visitors.

As it had been last night, her hospital bed was slightly elevated at the head. Earlier, Tina had helped her fix her hair into the tidy bun she preferred. She remained pale, but was more animated than she'd been in weeks. A good sign, suggesting the new course of treatment was beginning to have an effect.

"The man has to work," Sidney said. "You're lucky he stayed the night."

"I am that," G.G. said. She glanced at Tina. "*We* are."

Little did G.G. know. How to respond? While Tina considered her options, G.G. continued chatting, leaving her off the hook.

"Can you believe that man?" She placed her free hand over her chest. "Once this danged hip heals, I'm going to cook him a feast. Christmas dinner, too, if he'll come. Didn't I tell you he's special, Tina?"

"You did." Tina's cheeks warmed, and she knew she was blushing. Hoping no one noticed, she opened a tin of homemade gingersnaps Bob and Linda Sewell had sent with Rose, and offered one to G.G. She shook her head.

"He's an angel, for sure." Rose helped herself. "If I were thirty-five years younger…"

Sidney narrowed his eyes. "What's that supposed to mean?"

"Don't worry, Sidney." Rose chuckled. "I'm way too old for Ryan, so you're safe." She bit into the cookie and licked her lips appreciatively. "These are delicious. I'll have to get Linda's recipe."

"Alas, I'm too old, too." G.G. cast a sly look at Tina. "You, on the other hand—you're the perfect age for Ryan."

"G.G.!" Tina turned away from prying eyes to rearrange the flowers Sidney had brought. Had G.G. somehow guessed what had happened last night? Of course not, and thank heaven for that. Hands on her hips, she looked at the others and said, "Do you want me to focus on my career or not?"

"Well, of course that comes first," G.G. said.

"No question about it," Rose added.

Sidney nodded. "Like I always say, you'll be running that place in no time. Helping you with your education was the best investment I ever made."

Tina knew he was praising her, but the words only tightened the noose of obligation she imagined around her neck. Above all else, she must succeed in her career.

"Still," G.G. said, "you can't blame me for singing Ryan's praises."

Tina wondered how much longer Sidney and Rose planned to stay, and how she could steer the conversation elsewhere between now and then.

"Ryan this. Ryan that." Sidney scowled as he helped himself to two cookies. "This gushing drivel is making me sick. Could we talk about something else? Thanksgiving, for example. I ate so much, I about split my britches. Funny thing is, I'm hungry again."

He chomped on a gingersnap enthusiastically, and Tina silently thanked him for changing the subject.

"You didn't eat *that* much." Rose eyed him. "You're jealous, aren't you? Because you weren't here last night to help."

"Would've been, if Tina had let me know. Instead, she called *Ryan*. Why didn't you call me, Tina?"

She saw that she'd hurt the older man's feelings. In truth, the only person who'd come to mind had been Ryan. Of course, he was the youngest and healthiest male on the block. But the deep-down truth was, she'd wanted Ryan beside her.

"It was late and I knew you were asleep," she said.

"Ryan probably was sleeping, too," Sidney said. "He gets up with Maggie every morning, and he had to work today. Whereas I've been retired for years."

"Leave her alone, Sidney." Rose eyed him sternly.

"Ryan was the obvious choice," G.G. said. "He's young and strong, and Tina needed help getting me out of bed and into the car."

Tina nodded. "That's true." She hooked her arm through Sidney's and kissed his lined cheek. "I meant no offense."

"None taken, honey." He patted her arm. "I just want you to know you can count on me."

"Of course I know, and I truly appreciate you."

"Your flowers are just beautiful," G.G. said gently. "They certainly brighten up the room. Thank you, Sid."

His face reddened. "Figured you needed cheering up."

"I love my shawl, too, Rose. Put it around my shoulders, Tina."

Given G.G.'s discomfort, that wasn't so easy. But once Tina had managed the task, G.G. stroked the soft wool with a pleased smile. "Now I feel wrapped in friendship. Thank you so much."

"I was saving it for your Christmas present, but I'd rather you enjoy it now. The fuchsia color is perfect with your complexion."

Tina agreed.

Sidney pursed his lips. "When you're well—you're too pale now. I've seen you look better."

"Sidney!" Rose gave him a dirty look. "That's not very nice."

"But truthful," G.G. said. "He's right, I *have* had better days." Her face had begun to show the effects of this much conversation. "This isn't one of them. I think you'd better call the nurse, Tina."

Alarmed, Tina pushed the call button, then prepared to hustle the visitors out. "G.G. needs her rest."

That G.G. didn't argue only proved the point. "Thanks for traveling all this way for such a short visit," she said weakly.

"That's okay, I was coming anyway." Rose winked. "I'm moving my checking and savings accounts to the Halo Island Bank, and my bank here wants a signed note. So I'd planned this trip, anyway. Do you know that right now Halo Island Bank will deposit an extra twenty dollars into your savings when you open an account there? That bank has become a nicer place with Ryan running it. Won't he be surprised when I show up this afternoon?"

She looked quite pleased with herself.

Tina wondered what she'd do if she knew how Ryan really felt about the bank. He'd asked her to keep his feelings a secret, and she wasn't about to share. She would tell Ryan, though, when she saw him. Probably one last time before she left town. Her chest felt hollow, but now was no time to think about her broken heart.

"He'll be thrilled, I'm sure." G.G. managed a smile. "Maybe I'll do the same thing, once I feel better."

As Sidney and Rose started for the door, Rose glanced at Tina. "I meant to ask, who'll take care of G.G. when you leave?"

"She found me a full-time nurse," G.G. said before Tina could respond.

Afraid of the disapproval she might find in Rose and Sidney's faces, Tina glanced at the floor. "I could stay a few more days," she said.

"Nonsense." G.G. shook her finger. "With your new job starting Monday, I wouldn't dream of keeping you here."

"You definitely must go," Rose said.

"I'm with them." Sidney took Rose's arm and they moved toward the door.

"See?" G.G. said. "Everyone agrees. Besides, that nurse won't be with me for long. I'll be well in no time."

Chapter Fourteen

Where did all the paperwork come from? Sitting at his desk before a mound of it during a lull in an otherwise hectic Friday afternoon, Ryan rolled his tense shoulders. Who'd have guessed the day after Thanksgiving would be so busy? As soon as he'd walked in late this morning, Jason had gone home. Flu, he said. Danielle had gone home sick, too, and Ryan and Serena were scrambling.

Which was especially bad, since Ryan didn't want to be here, either. He was exhausted and very worried about Maggie, who was at Norma's for the day.

While he and Tina had lost themselves in the best sex of his life, Maggie had screamed herself and Norma awake time and again. With Tina about to leave, Ryan had known this would happen. No telling how G.G.'s being in the hospital would affect his daughter. He supposed he'd find out tonight.

On the ferry ride from Anacortes, he'd called Dr. Dove and then Dr. Wright, the family therapist whom Dr. Dove had recommended. Lucky for him and Maggie, she was right here on the island. He'd scheduled the earliest available appointment, which was next week. First for him in the morning—Dr. Wright required that. Ryan didn't mind.

He needed help and a game plan. Maggie's appointment was later the same day, after school.

Ryan yawned, so tired that his eyes watered, then sipped his coffee. If all that wasn't enough to worry about, Beale had sent a branch-wide e-mail today instead of waiting until Monday. *You Are Still Behind*, the subject line read.

Ryan had read the negative message with growing frustration. Had Beale heard one word Ryan had said to him? Apparently not, for there wasn't a single "atta boy/girl" in the whole thing, only criticism and more dire warnings. No wonder Jason and Danielle had gone home "sick." He wouldn't be surprised if they both quit.

Not about to put up with any more of his boss's crap, Ryan had called his office, only to be told by Beale's secretary that the man wanted to see Ryan first thing Monday morning. Which sounded ominous, and since corporate offices were in Anacortes it meant an early ferry ride.

Ryan figured the man meant to fire him. Well, he just might one-up the guy and resign first.

Yeah, he'd assured his staff he'd stay. But that was before this. *Hell.* Scowling, he riffled through the papers on his desk. For two cents, he'd…

Open your own bank, said a voice in his head.

"No sweat," he muttered. Uh-huh. That'd sure help Maggie.

Suddenly, Rose Thorne marched into his office. "Hello, Ryan. My, the bank is busy today."

"A couple of my staff are out sick." He gestured her toward the chair opposite his desk. "This is a nice surprise. What brings you here?"

"Several things. Sidney and I visited G.G. this morning, apparently right after you left. Sorry we missed you."

Ryan wasn't. This morning he'd been in no mood to see any of the neighbors.

"You should've heard G.G. and Tina talking about you. Were your ears burning?"

"What'd they say?" Ryan asked, curious about Tina.

"Only that you're a wonderful man."

"They did, huh?" That made him feel good.

That word—*wonderful*—reminded him about other pretty amazing things. Tina naked, and their hot, mind-blowing sex. His body tightened, and he knew he'd best not stand up just now. Shifting in his chair, he wished to hell he could forget about making love with her. No point in wanting more of what was over and done with.

"Guess what else?" Rose said. "G.G.'s doctor says she can come home tomorrow. They'll be on the noon ferry. Isn't modern medicine amazing?"

"Sure is." He stifled a yawn.

Oblivious, Rose chattered on. "Did you know Tina hired a nurse, who'll start Sunday afternoon? That way she won't have to miss any more work. Smart girl, our Tina."

Too bad she was so damned focused on her career, because if she stayed on the island instead… The thought confused Ryan. Tina was all wrong for him, and he didn't want a relationship, anyway. Neither did she. No matter how good they were together in bed, what they'd shared was for one night, period.

Yet knowing she'd be back on the island tomorrow, and for one more night—already he looked forward to that, wondering whether he'd find a way to get her alone. He caught himself and set his jaw. *Dammit, it's over.*

"Since Tina and G.G. don't have a car with them, Sidney will ferry his car over and pick them up." Rose lowered her voice. "His feelings were hurt when Tina called you instead of him last night. That's why she asked him to drive."

Ryan almost wished she *had* called the older man. Then he wouldn't be sitting here now, lusting after her and wanting more. Which was a damned lie. He'd lusted after her ever since he'd first met her at the potluck.

"Sidney's a nice guy," he said.

"So are you."

Rose was waiting for him to speak, so he nodded. Enough already. "I know you didn't stop in just to tell me about G.G."

"You're right. I have exciting news for you." Looking delighted, she dug into her enormous purse and pulled out a check. "I saw in the paper that Halo Island Bank is offering a twenty-dollar bonus to open a checking-and-savings account. That, and the lovely fact that you now run this bank, have convinced me. I'm moving my accounts here."

"You don't want to do that."

"What?"

Her jaw dropped, but she was no more surprised than Ryan. What the hell was the matter with him?

"From a financial perspective it's not a good idea, that's all," he said. "What if you decide you don't like banking here?"

"As long as you're in charge, I'll like it fine." She looked confused. "I've never heard of a bank manager discouraging a willing customer from transferring her account to his bank."

"You have now. If I were you, I'd keep two accounts, one here and one at your bank in Anacortes. If, after a few months, you're happy here, then close out the other one."

"But I already closed everything there." Rose looked upset. "They gave me a cashier's check. I can't very well undo what's done. I just wish I'd talked to you first. Or listened to Sidney. He said I was being impulsive." She gave Ryan a frightened look. "Do you think so?"

"Not to worry," he soothed. "This is a reputable bank and everything will be fine. Let me grab a signature card and we'll get you started. Would you like a cup of coffee?"

"No, thanks."

Moments later, Ryan returned with the card. While Rose filled in the necessary information, he opened the new-account program on his computer. He was tired, and when he yawned Rose looked up from the paperwork.

"Norma's tired, too," she said. "I heard about Maggie's nightmares. I'm sorry they're so bad."

So Norma had told her. Well, his daughter's sleep problems were not exactly a secret. Ryan rubbed the knots in the back of his neck. "I'm sorry, too."

"That child needs a mommy."

First Tina, and now Rose. "We're doing okay, thanks." Ryan clamped his jaw, in effect warning her to stay out of his business. "You about done with that signature card?"

"Just about."

Rose returned the form, and Ryan thought about Tina. They were supposed to act as if nothing had happened between them. Pretend he'd never seen her naked, had never touched and tasted every inch of her body, and never watched her come apart? That wasn't going to be easy. Especially when what he wanted most was to make love with her again.

All in all, it was a bad situation.

Behind his eyes, a headache threatened. He rubbed his forehead.

Rose handed him the completed signature card. "That was real sweet of you to go with Tina and G.G. to Anacortes." She eyed him shrewdly, making him wonder whether she knew something.

"Any neighbor would." Not wanting to revisit the subject again, Ryan stood up. "Sit tight," he said. "I'll be right back with a receipt and your savings and check books."

As he headed across the lobby, he caught a whiff of coconut. His body went on red alert and he almost stumbled. But Tina was at the hospital in Anacortes. Apparently someone in the lobby used the same shampoo.

Wanting Tina was driving him nuts and making him miserable. As he neared Serena's window, several customers, unhappy waiting in a long line, frowned at him. If he'd known how to be a teller, he'd have stepped in. But that was a skill he'd never been taught.

By now, a full-scale headache pounded his temples.

The day just kept going downhill.

"WE'RE ALMOST home," Sidney said as he slowed to turn onto Huckleberry Hill Road.

The hospital had released G.G. later than planned, and instead of taking the noon ferry they'd had to catch the three-fifty. Now, at five, it was dark and rainy. Cheery light glowed from the windows of most houses in the neighborhood.

Tina studiously avoided glancing at the well-lit house near the end of the cul-de-sac. Knowing Ryan was inside it, she felt oddly nervous, her stomach fluttery and her heart thudding with anticipation—all without so much as a glimpse of the man.

And for what? The things they had shared were behind them now. Which was the wisest course. Tina hated to leave G.G., yet at the same time she was anxious to get back to Seattle. Maybe then she'd be able to breathe normally again. It would be far easier than acting as if she had no feelings for Ryan.

Her certainty that once she left the island she'd eventually move beyond loving him was what was keeping her strong. She only hoped her friendship with Maggie survived.

Suddenly, the rain turned into a furious storm, pounding the roof of the car so fiercely she couldn't even hear herself think.

"Goodness me," G.G. said. "Isn't this something?"

"I hope it lets up before we get out of the car," Tina said.

"Doesn't look as if it will." With the windshield wipers sweeping madly across the windshield, Sidney rolled slowly up G.G.'s driveway.

"I don't mind." G.G. let out a happy sigh that was audible over the rain. "It's good to be home again."

The instant Sidney braked to a stop, Tina opened her door. "You and Sidney stay where you are, while I get an umbrella."

Pelted by rain, she dashed up the walkway. By the time she unlocked the front door, she was soaking wet.

The house still smelled like Thanksgiving, and Tina's stomach growled. She'd fix leftovers tonight. Seconds later, she opened an umbrella and hurried back to the car.

Despite what Tina had said, Sidney had the passenger door open and was already trying to help G.G. out. She wasn't as strong as she'd been before the infection had set in and she couldn't rotate her body in the seat, let alone help Sidney pull her up.

Tina handed him the umbrella and tried the same tactics she'd used previously to help G.G. out of bed. But that didn't work, either. Neither of them was strong enough to move the woman. They needed help.

"Tina, go knock on Ryan's door," G.G. said. "And hurry

up. I've got to use the bathroom. Sidney, get back in the car before you're soaked to the bone."

Tina held the umbrella over Sidney, who closed G.G.'s door and got back into the front seat. Then, ready or not, it was time to face Ryan.

Moments later, sanding under the eaves of his big front porch, she set down the open umbrella. The porch light was off, and it was dark. With a cold, wet hand she knocked on the door, breathless from more than just rushing over. The rhythm of the rain tattooing against the roof matched the rapid beat of her heart.

Maggie's face peered through the living room curtains. She squealed, although the sound was muffled through the door. "Daddy, it's Tina! Can I let her in?"

The porch light flashed on, and shortly afterward the door swung open. Maggie stood on the threshold, Ryan behind her.

Before Tina uttered a word, the little girl hurled herself forward. Laughing, she hugged Tina's legs and buried her face against her hips. "You came back! Ew, you're cold and wet, but I don't care!"

"I certainly am." Tina laughed, too, and her heart melted. How she adored this child. Oh, she would miss her.

Over Maggie's head, she glanced at Ryan. He looked as exhausted as she felt. The corners of his generous mouth turned downward and his eyes were dark and brooding. Because she was hugging Maggie, accepting and encouraging her love?

Tina loosened the little girl's grip, squatted down and peered soberly into her face. "I'm still leaving tomorrow, sweetie. I'll be back for Christmas, but after that, you and I won't see much of each other."

Ryan's nod of approval assured her that she'd said the

right thing. As she stood again, his gaze held hers, and for a moment she couldn't look away. Behind his concerns for Maggie, another emotion flared in his eyes and face. Sexual desire. For her.

Heaven help her, her body quivered. Her nerves tensed and stood on end, and she strained toward him without actually moving a muscle. Feigning disinterest, hiding her love and desire, was agony. Impossible.

She jerked her gaze away, the breath escaping from her lips, thin and wispy, in the cold air. G.G. was waiting.

"Sidney and I are having trouble getting G.G. out of the car," she said. "We need your help."

Ryan nodded, seeming relieved to know that her reason for showing up on his doorstep was not about them.

"I'll be right back," he told Maggie.

"I want to come, too."

"In this rain? Better not. You watch out the window."

Tina tipped up Maggie's chin. "If your daddy doesn't mind, I'll come over tomorrow and say goodbye. Would that be okay?"

"Is it okay, Daddy?"

"Sure, Sunshine."

Maggie brightened and Tina felt better. "G.G.'s waiting for us. I'll see you later," she said.

"I'll be right back, Maggie."

Without grabbing a coat or waiting for a reply from his daughter, Ryan slipped out behind Tina and closed the door. Tina reached for the umbrella.

"I'll take that." His warm fingers brushed her icy ones.

They crowded together underneath it. Heat and love rippled in waves through Tina, and she fought to keep from leaning into Ryan's solid strength.

She glanced up at him. In the dark his eyes were black

and shadowed, but she felt their intensity and sensed his pain. "Are you okay?"

"Maggie's nightmares are worse than ever," he said in an anguished voice as they moved toward the street.

Tina felt bad for both man and child. "Because of me?"

"And G.G. This hospitalization—well, it scared her."

"It scared us all," Tina said. "But G.G.'s okay now. Maggie understands that, right?"

"She says she does, but she's said that before and she didn't. Who knows what's really in her five-year-old mind?"

Tina did. Guilt and self-blame, for things that were absolutely not her fault. Afraid of making Ryan feel even worse, she kept quiet.

"I scheduled an appointment with a therapist. We're meeting her on Wednesday."

"I'm glad, Ryan. I wish someone had done that for me. I hope it helps."

"You and me both."

"How are you holding up?" he asked as they reached the street.

I'm in love with you, and my heart is breaking. "Relieved that G.G.'s out of the hospital and finally on her way to recovery," she said.

They waited while a car rolled by, splashing water from a street puddle.

"How are *you?*" she asked. *Do you wish I was staying on the island as much as I do?*

"It's been a crappy few days. Besides dealing with Maggie, I've been summoned to corporate headquarters on Monday. They're not happy with our bottom line. My guess is, they're going to fire me."

"What? But you're the best manager that bank has ever had. Everyone says so."

"The board doesn't care about that. They're only interested in the numbers. Don't say anything, all right?"

"You know I won't. I'm sorry, Ryan."

"Don't be. I've been thinking about resigning, anyway."

"You should, and then you should open your own bank. Like you said you wanted to."

"We had this conversation before," he said, setting his jaw. "Maggie's my priority."

"Right." They crossed the street. "What time should I stop by tomorrow to say goodbye to her?"

"What time are you leaving?"

"Early afternoon, after the nurse arrives."

"Come right before you go."

"Okay."

After that, there was nothing left to say. As they headed up the driveway only the gravel crunching under their feet filled the heavy silence.

WHEN TINA TRUDGED toward Ryan's door the next afternoon, dark clouds obscured the sky. Her spirits were just as dark.

Before she could knock, he opened the door. "Maggie's upstairs, making you a card," he said.

"How is she?"

His desolate expression said it all. "How do you think?"

"I'm sorry, Ryan." How she wished she could stay here with him and Maggie.

"We'll be okay. And once we see that therapist Wednesday…"

"Will you let me know how that goes?"

He nodded. Then bracketed his mouth with his hand and turned toward the stairs. "Maggie, Tina's here, and she needs to catch the ferry."

Footsteps pattered overhead. Clutching a folded sheet

of construction paper and dressed in her princess dress, Maggie flew down the stairs.

"You're all dressed up," Tina said.

"Uh-huh. 'Cause you're leaving and I wanted to look pretty for you." She held out the paper shyly. "I made this for you."

The card was glittery and covered with crayon drawings. "This is beautiful."

"I know. That's you and me and Daddy," Maggie pointed to the crudely drawn stick figures. "And Eggwhite in her cage. Now you won't forget us."

"Oh, honey." Tears filled Tina's eyes. "I could never forget you."

She knelt down and opened her arms. Maggie fell into them.

They shared a warm hug. When Maggie let her go, she was round-eyed and sober. "Will you call me on the telephone?"

"If that's okay with your daddy."

Tina glanced up at Ryan. His hands were shoved into his jeans' pockets and his eyes were bleak.

"Tina will be very busy with her job."

"Not too busy for a phone call now and then," she said.

"We'll see. Say goodbye to Tina, Sunshine. I want to talk to her privately."

"Thank you again for the card," Tina said. "I'll keep it on my desk, where I'll see it every day." She meant that, too. Once more, she hugged Maggie, then kissed her little cheek. "I'll see you at Christmas."

"Go on upstairs, Maggie. I'll be up shortly."

When Maggie had disappeared, Ryan turned to Tina. He spoke in a voice too low to carry beyond them.

"You shouldn't have said you'd call when you know you'll be too busy and too wrapped up in your work."

"Not for Maggie, I won't. I promise."

"I'll hold you to it, then."

He cupped her cheek. Bent down and brushed his mouth over her lips, a soft, sweet kiss she felt clear to her toes. When he released her, his eyes were dark with feeling.

"Goodbye, Tina."

"See you at Christmas," she said.

He opened his mouth. Closed it. Rubbed the back of his neck, then opened the door.

Feeling as if her heart had splintered into jagged pieces, she walked away.

Chapter Fifteen

Monday morning, Ryan sat in front of Bernard Beale's mahogany desk at corporate headquarters. Wearing a tailored suit and a friendly expression, Beale looked successful and friendly like a snake about to strike. Ryan was ready, his own expression neutral.

"You're probably wondering why I invited you here," Beale said.

"To fire me, I expect, but before you do you'll hear me out. Yes, Halo Island Bank's bottom line is lower than your projections, and though I've only worked for you five months I accept responsibility for the numbers. But part of the problem belongs to you and the board. My staff members are competent and hardworking, and I praise them constantly. But without money and recognition from you, it's not enough. If you acknowledged their efforts and offered training and incentives, I'm confident we could turn the bank around. But you don't, and they feel unappreciated. The end result is poor customer service. Unhappy customers take their business elsewhere, and business spirals downward."

Beale opened his mouth, but Ryan held up his hand, stopping him. "I'm almost finished. I can no longer work for a company with your values. You can't fire me, because as of today I'm giving my notice." He pulled a letter of resignation from his briefcase. "Please share that with the board."

"Hold on a minute, Ryan."

"I can leave now, or in two weeks." What he'd do with his time was anybody's guess. But resigning felt like the right thing to do.

"You've got it all wrong." Beale shook his head. "I had no intention of firing you. I invited you here to let you in on something that won't become public knowledge until next week. So keep what I'm about to tell you under wraps." He paused, and Ryan nodded. "The first of next year, we're putting Halo Island Bank on the market. Given your background, I thought you might be interested in buying it. Then you can do whatever you want with it."

Ryan had never expected this. "You're selling?"

Beale nodded. "We've decided to cut our losses and consolidate. Are you interested in buying the bank?"

Hell, yes. But Maggie came first. With genuine regret, Ryan shook his head. "No, thanks."

"Suit yourself. I hate to lose you, Ryan." Beale blew out a breath. "However, if you insist on resigning, I'll accept this letter—provided you stay on through December. This time of year, it'd be impossible to find a replacement."

Ryan figured he could hold out for another month. That would give him time to break the news to Jason, Danielle and Serena, and to figure out what to do with the rest of his life.

He nodded. "Agreed. Please don't announce my resignation until I talk with my staff. I'll let you know when I've done that."

He left the building wishing he could share what had happened with Tina. But she'd gone back to work today, and Ryan doubted she wanted to hear from him. He had no illusions that with her new responsibilities she'd soon forget about him and Maggie.

Sure, she'd said she'd call Maggie. Once, he figured, before work took over her life.

Now that she was gone, Ryan meant to forget her, too, and move on. Period. Christmas was a month away, and he was certain that by then this Tina thing would be behind him.

As she'd promised, Tina stood at Jim Sperling's side Monday morning. The entire staff of CE Marketing was crowded into the reception area, some still not quite awake this first day back from the Thanksgiving holiday, assembled for a hastily called meeting.

"I have an important announcement to make." Her boss smiled at her fondly. "Please join me in welcoming our new creative director, Tina Morrell."

He applauded, and everyone followed suit—even Kendra. Though her smile looked forced.

"Thank you all," Tina said. "I'm pleased and excited to have this wonderful opportunity."

Surrounded by friends and colleagues, she almost believed herself.

Following the announcement, Jim went into CEO mode. "All right, people, we have a business to run. Let's get to it."

As Tina headed with June toward her office, which they were about to pack up and exchange for a bigger, corner space, she wondered what had happened with Ryan's meeting at bank headquarters. Had he resigned, and if so, what would he do next? And how was Maggie? Had she slept badly again?

She wanted to call and talk to the little girl today, but if she meant to get over Ryan, it might make more sense to wait a while. Besides, she didn't want to crowd him. She would call in a few days, she decided. Until then, she'd have to get her information from G.G.

For now, she had an ad department to run.

RYAN TOOK Wednesday morning off to meet with Dr. Patricia Wright, the specialist Dr. Dove had recommended. "A whiz with children and their parents," he'd said. Preoccupied with today's appointment, Ryan hadn't yet told his staff he was resigning. He figured he'd do that sometime next week, around the time the board announced that the bank was for sale.

As he drove across town, his windshield wipers swished in vain against the pouring rain. Compared to L.A., winters in the Pacific Northwest were gray and rough on a man's spirits, but he didn't think about that today. He actually looked forward to talking with Dr. Wright. Anything to help Maggie.

Minutes later, he was standing in the therapist's office, shaking her hand. She was an attractive blonde of indeterminate age, with a firm grip.

Her office looked friendly enough—there was an oriental rug over the carpet and cream-colored leather furniture. Nice pictures on the wall, and a small potted tree in the corner of the room, as homey as someone's living room. Ryan wouldn't have cared if they'd met in a broom closet.

"Please, sit down." Dr. Wright gestured toward two armchairs separated by a glass coffee table. "Would you like coffee?"

This wasn't a social visit, and he shook his head. Took

his seat, and cleared his throat. "How does this therapy stuff work?"

"We talk, that's all." Looking relaxed and ready to listen, she smiled. "Tell me about Maggie."

Since the therapist already knew Maggie's age and that she was in kindergarten and an only child, Ryan went right to the critical information. "She's had a rough life."

He told Dr. Wright everything—about his impending divorce from Heidi and her tragic death when Maggie was eighteen months old. The break-off of his engagement last year, when his fiancée had chosen a job in Texas over him and Maggie. How Mrs. Miumi, who'd been around since Maggie was born, had left soon after that to care for her grandson.

"Every female she ever loved disappeared from her life," he said. Dr. Wright gave a sympathetic nod, and he continued. "After Mrs. Miumi left last spring, I decided to sell my business so that I could spend more time with Maggie. Halo Island seemed to be a great place to raise kids, so we moved here. Now I work a job with regular hours, and Maggie and I are together every night and on weekends."

Maybe he should tell her about his resignation. "The job I took isn't working out, though. As of the first of next year, I'll be unemployed."

"We'll get to that later. Tell me more about Maggie."

He nodded. "We're in an excellent neighborhood, and she seems to enjoy living on the island. She likes her teacher and her school, in general, and she's made friends."

"That all sounds fine. But you're not here because things are going well."

The woman was right. Ryan drew in a breath and then let it out. "After Heidi died, Maggie started waking up crying. Nightmares. They flare up whenever someone she loves leaves. Lately, she's been waking up a lot, sometimes two and three times in one night."

"Do you have any idea why?"

He hesitated, wondering how much to say. Therapists weren't supposed to talk about their patients, but what if Dr. Wright did?

"If you don't think you can trust me, Ryan, maybe you should find a different therapist."

He gave her a humorless grin. "What are you, a mind reader?"

"After years of practice, I'm pretty good at reading people. Now, why don't you tell me what's going on."

"The woman across the street—her name is G.G.—is like the grandma Maggie never had. She watches her after school and spends a lot of time with her. A month ago, she had hip surgery. While she recuperated, she needed help, so…"

He told Dr. Wright about Tina, and Maggie's immediate attachment to her. He explained about Eggwhite escaping and G.G.'s emergency trip to the hospital, and about Tina's promotion. He told Dr. Wright everything, except what had happened that night in Anacortes. That was private.

"Maggie's crazy about Tina," he said. "And even though both Tina and I reminded her often that Tina wouldn't be staying long on the island, she didn't understand. The multiple nightmares started around the time Tina left on Sunday," he finished. "I know they're directly related to her leaving and to G.G.'s stay in the hospital. For some reason Maggie thinks Tina left because she did something wrong. Tina promised to call Maggie, which probably will help, and G.G.'s better now. But the nightmares keep coming." He made a helpless gesture with his hands. "I don't know how to help my daughter. That's why I'm here."

Dr. Wright offered no advice, just silently jotted down notes.

Impatient, Ryan shifted in his chair. "Any ideas?"

Her pen stilled. She looked at him without judgment or pity. "I'll know more after I talk with Maggie this afternoon. Let's talk more about *you* now. Tell me about this job you're leaving and what you want to do with the rest of your life."

BY THE TIME Ryan and Maggie left Dr. Wright's on Wednesday afternoon it was almost dark, but at least the rain had stopped. Work had been a bitch, and Ryan was sure Jason would give his two weeks' notice any day now. He'd called a branch meeting for Monday to announce his own resignation and to share the news that, come next year, Halo Island Bank would be up for sale.

In no mood to cook dinner, he glanced at his daughter. "What do you say we stop at the drive-through for burgers and fries tonight?"

"I say, awesome!" Maggie bounced in her seat, bumping against the seat belt. "Can we listen to the radio on the way?"

"Sure." Ryan turned to an oldies station, her favorite.

While she sang along off-key, acting like her usual bubbly self, Ryan counted his blessings. Meeting with Dr. Wright hadn't upset her nearly as much as he'd feared it might.

He reviewed his and the therapist's final conversation, had while Maggie played with one of her assistants in a different room.

"Your daughter is a resilient little girl," Dr. Wright had said. "Children often blame themselves for everything that happens, however, and that's what Maggie has done. Yet despite losing her mother and other women in her life, she remains cheerful and happy."

"Except when she sleeps," Ryan had replied.

"We'll discuss that shortly. The one constant in her life is you. You're also the most important person in her world. That is the basis for her well-being—she knows that no matter what happens, her daddy will always be there for her."

That was good to know. "That's the plan."

Ryan had barely let out a relieved breath, before the therapist continued.

"However, because you're the center of Maggie's life, when you're not happy, neither is she. Right or wrong, she blames herself."

Hadn't Tina said the same thing? "I'm happy enough," he'd said, knowing that Dr. Wright didn't necessarily buy that. Too bad because he wasn't about to get into his personal issues. "What can I do to help my daughter?"

"Every child craves a mother's love, and Maggie is no different. It's normal for her to form an attachment to a woman around the age her mother would be if she were alive, especially if the woman genuinely cares about her. For that reason, I'd be surprised if she *didn't* grieve now that Tina has gone."

Get happy and find a mother figure for Maggie. A while back Tina had given him the same advice. *Well, hell.* He could've saved the time and money and skipped the therapy.

"I suggest you talk about Tina often, and continue to re-inforce the message that she left for reasons that have nothing to do with Maggie."

"Talk about her?"

Dr. Wright had nodded. "It's an important way to ac-knowledge her entirely valid feelings and get her to open up to you."

"Tina promised Maggie she'd call now and then, but

she's busy with her career. Even though she has good intentions, I'm not sure she'll follow through."

"If she doesn't call you, then you call her. That way Maggie won't feel that Tina has deserted her. And Ryan, I suggest you seriously consider buying the bank."

This had dumbfounded him. Sure, he'd told her how much he enjoyed building and running his own bank, but he'd also let her know that Maggie came first. He frowned. "But that would mean hours and hours away from Maggie."

"I'm certain you and she can work that out. You're far too young to retire. Without a career that makes you happy…"

"I know, I know. If I'm unhappy, Maggie will be, too."

Ryan wanted to discuss the whole thing with Tina. Damn, but he missed her. He wasn't calling her, though. Not until Maggie asked him to.

The song on the radio ended and his daughter glanced at him.

"Dr. Wright taught me what to do when I have a bad dream."

The therapist had explained this to Ryan, too, but he wanted to hear Maggie's version, to find out whether she understood. "What did she say?" he asked, slowing to make a turn.

"That I can make the bad things stop. I just stamp my foot and say, 'I don't like you, go away!' and the mean people will."

Such a simple technique. Maggie sounded quite pleased about it, and Ryan only hoped it worked. "If you're asleep, how can you do that?" he asked, wanting to know.

"Practice, practice, practice," she said, parroting Dr. Wright. "If I really want to get rid of those mean people in my dreams, I can."

"I believe you, Maggie."

"Good, 'cause I'm gonna do it."

The way she raised her chin reminded him of Tina. Copying her gestures? Man, was she attached. Ryan hoped the therapist was right about Maggie being able to stop the dreams and that she would quickly get used to life without Tina.

A new song started. Singing along, Maggie turned to look out at the darkness. Ryan went back to thinking about the rest of the afternoon's conversation with Dr. Wright.

"Maggie won't be getting a mother," he'd said. "My track record with women has been lousy." He thought about Tina, who was basically gone from their lives. She might be back for the holidays, but like all the women he'd cared for, her career came first. "I'm not about to put my daughter's heart at risk again for any woman."

"Fine, but if you meet the right woman, and she loves both you and Maggie, why not take a chance at happiness?"

Chapter Sixteen

"Is it all right to clean in here, Miss Morrell?"

Tina looked up from the computer screen, where she was putting together numbers for a presentation. She smiled at the janitor. "Certainly, Henry. I need a break, anyway."

She glanced at the card Maggie had given her, which occupied a prominent position on the corner of her desk. The little girl was doing well. The nightmares were less frequent now. Tina received daily reports from G.G., who, having made a quick recovery following her hospital stay, was back to watching her after school.

Stretching, Tina headed down the empty hallways of CE Marketing. The last one here, as usual. Especially this time of year. With only two weeks until Christmas, business was slowing down, and everyone was preoccupied with holiday activities.

Since Tina had finished her shopping the weekend before and had no family here, she was happy to stay at work. She was still settling into her new job, and with so much to do, and the office closed from next Friday until January 2, she could use the extra time to catch up.

In the fifteen days since she'd assumed the title of

creative director, she'd made a habit of arriving at the office early in the morning and leaving late. The long hours and breakneck pace kept her way too busy to think.

Yet for the first time in her life, work failed to distract her from the gaping hole in her heart. Every day she grew more dissatisfied and unhappy, and every day she worked harder in an effort to stifle her feelings. As a result, she was sleeping badly and now had a bear of an ulcer. She'd had to give up coffee altogether and had switched from over-the-counter antacids to a high-strength prescription medication.

Too bad no one had invented a pill for heartache. Tina missed Ryan and Maggie—and G.G. and Kate and the rest of her friends and neighbors on Halo Island.

At least she'd talked with Maggie and Ryan a few times. She'd called them twice. They'd called her, too, Maggie always talking first and then handing the phone to Ryan.

The difference in their tones was telling. While Maggie was sweet and chatty and full of news, Ryan was more reserved. He did mention that he'd resigned and was looking into various options, but with Maggie nearby he never said much. And he never called without his daughter nearby. Well, he didn't want a relationship.

Crossing the reception area, which was festively decorated with holly, poinsettias and a tall artificial tree, Tina moved to a large window overlooking downtown Seattle. Staring out at the darkness and the lights of the bustling city below, she felt as if life were passing her by. The one positive was that G.G. and the others were proud and pleased about her job.

That's what matters most. Wasn't it? Suddenly needing to hear G.G.'s reassuring voice, Tina pulled her cell phone from her blazer pocket and called.

"What a pleasant surprise," G.G. said, sounding much

more like her old, energetic self. "You just missed Ryan and Maggie. That sweet man stopped by tonight to bring my Christmas decorations down from the attic. He offered to string the outdoor lights tomorrow."

The mere mention of Ryan's name made Tina's heart ache. "That's very considerate of him."

"Yes, it is. I promised Maggie I'd save decorating the tree for after school tomorrow. We'll hang the ornaments and tinsel, and then have Christmas cookies and cocoa, the way you and I used to do. Won't that be fun?"

No doubt Maggie's boundless enthusiasm would add special magic to the festivities. "You're making me feel extremely nostalgic," Tina said. "I wish I could be there."

She loved the December holidays, but never bothered to decorate her Seattle apartment. What for, when she always spent Christmas on Halo Island—the only place that had ever really mattered? "How was your checkup today with Dr. Lomax?"

"Excellent. You'll never guess—I've graduated to a cane now. No more walker! He says that by the time you're home again, I'll be walking without any help at all."

"But that's only a week from Friday. You're doing so well."

G.G. chuckled. "I know, and I'm tickled. You didn't ask about the Rosses' potluck last night. It was great fun, but of course we all missed you. We toasted you and your promotion—even Maggie. Of course, her eggnog was alcohol-free."

In her mind, Tina pictured her friends and loved ones, laughing and talking and sharing their holiday plans. And felt even more wistful. "Sorry I missed that."

"We all understand, honey. Your career comes first."

Which Tina knew all too well. She sighed.

"What is it, dear?"

"Nothing. It's been a long day."

"You're still at the office, aren't you?"

"I'm afraid so."

"You've always given your all to the job. That's how you got where you are. Did you take the time to have dinner tonight?"

"I had a sandwich." Purchased from a vending machine in the company lunchroom.

"That's not much of a meal. Go home, dear. The work will keep."

If she went home, she'd only feel lonely. "I will. Soon."

"I'll bet you're looking forward to the company party on Friday night."

Every year Jim Sperling treated his employees to a catered dinner party at an exclusive club, followed by an evening of entertainment. Always good fun.

"I am," Tina said. Even if she didn't have a date. "You should see the glittery cocktail dress I bought."

"E-mail me some pictures, or better yet bring the dress with you next week. Who are you taking?"

"Um, nobody."

"No one to appreciate that new outfit? That seems a shame." G.G. made a sympathetic noise. "You know, if you invited Ryan, he'd escort you."

A "pity" escort? No, thank you. "He doesn't date, remember?"

"It's not as if you're asking him to marry you, Tina. For goodness' sake, this is your Christmas party. Ask him as a friend, dear. It'll give me a chance to have Maggie all to myself for the whole night. We'll have a slumber party."

G.G. didn't know they'd made love—or that they'd agreed to forget the whole thing. She didn't realize that

Tina was in love with Ryan, and that he didn't want her love. Or that she was trying hard to get over him.

"I can't do that." It was time to end the conversation. "I should probably get back to work."

"All right, but first tell me, how are things with Kendra?"

She and Tina would never be friends, but Tina respected her coworker more each day. "Better, thanks. I think she's finally getting used to me as her boss. She's a hard worker, and very creative."

"That's good to hear. Take care of yourself, honey, and let's talk again soon."

ONE WEEK after his appointment with Dr. Wright, Ryan headed home, glad the workday was over. As he'd been expecting for days, this morning Jason and Danielle had given their two weeks' notice. Having tendered his own resignation, he didn't blame them. Serena, who was a single mom, needed her job too much to quit, but Ryan figured that once she lined something else up, she'd leave, too.

Then it was anybody's guess what would happen to Halo Island Bank.

They were good employees, and if Ryan bought the bank he'd hire back all three, give them raises and set up a solid incentive-pay program.

If. He hadn't figured out how to do that without neglecting Maggie. If not for Dr. Wright's advice, he'd have completely dismissed the idea. He still might.

He was almost at Huckleberry Hill Road now, and looking forward to stringing G.G.'s house lights. He'd done his own the previous weekend. Thanks to a timer, his place was lit up now.

Ryan pulled into his garage and parked, then crossed his front yard. Tonight, G.G. had left her drapes open, and he stopped in the middle of the yard and watched as his daughter hung tinsel on G.G.'s artificial tree. He couldn't see her face, but her mouth was moving. By the way she jumped and pranced around, he knew she was happy.

Buoyed by the knowledge, he smiled, shook his head and strolled toward the street. Now that Maggie knew how to stop the bad dreams, she was doing well, far better than he'd expected. She missed Tina, but any time she wanted to talk about her, which was often, Ryan followed their therapist's advice and listened. That seemed to help, and so did the phone calls.

As busy as Tina was, she hadn't forgotten to call Maggie, for which Ryan was grateful. He still missed her, way more than he should. Which she'd never know. He had no delusions about her missing him. According to G.G., she really liked her new job and was putting in long hours. Before she'd even left, he'd figured she would.

Come next Friday, a little over a week from now, she'd be back on the island for Christmas. Pathetic, how he looked forward to that.

Man, did he have it bad. If he didn't know himself better he'd think he was in love with her.

But he absolutely did not love her. *The hell you say,* argued a voice in his head. *You are so whipped, it isn't funny.*

Dammit, it was true. Halfway up G.G.'s walkway he stopped and smacked his forehead. Of all the ridiculous things to happen. Once again he'd tangled himself up with a woman who put her career above all else.

When would he ever learn?

Hands in his pockets, muttering choice epithets at himself, he trudged to the front stoop.

Before he even reached the door, G.G. opened it. Christmas music spilled out, filling the air.

"Hello, Ryan," she said. "Maggie's in the washroom, and I want to talk to you before she comes out. Let's go into the den and get those lights."

Alarmed by the notion that maybe something had gone wrong with his daughter, Ryan followed. Using her cane, G.G. breezed ahead. She was recovering amazingly fast.

The second they entered the den, she closed the door and turned to him. "I'm worried about Tina."

"Tina?" So this wasn't about Maggie. He let out a relieved breath. Then he looked at G.G. "What's going on?"

"After you and Maggie left last night, she called. From work. Seven-thirty and she was still at it. Working all those hours? It isn't healthy." G.G. pursed her lips and shook her head. "And don't even get me started about the flare-up of her ulcer. I don't think she's happy at all, Ryan."

He disagreed. "Last time we talked, she sounded like she was. She was real busy then, too." Too busy to spare more than a few minutes of her time.

"I've known her since she was in kindergarten, so I know her pretty well. No matter what she says, there's something wrong. I think she's homesick, but I don't know for sure." G.G. sighed. "Whatever it is, she isn't about to confide in me. But you—I know you can find out what's bothering her."

"Me? What makes you think she'd tell me?"

"Call it an old lady's hunch. Now, it just so happens that she needs a date for her company Christmas party on Friday night. You could take her and get her to open up."

He didn't date, especially when there wasn't a prayer that anything good would come of it. But G.G.'s eager look and his own deep feelings for Tina were too much to fight. "You think I should invite myself?"

"I do. Maggie can stay with me. We'll make ginger-bread boys and watch a movie in bed. It'll be fun."

Ryan figured his daughter would enjoy that. Suddenly, he couldn't wait to see Tina. Lay his heart on the line and tell her he loved her. Scary as that was. If she rejected him… He couldn't feel much worse than he did now. At least it'd be in Seattle, safely away from Maggie.

"Can those lights wait another day?" he asked. "Before I call Tina, I want to go home and talk things over with Maggie."

G.G. beamed. "That sounds like a fine idea."

Maggie's footsteps pattered over the carpet, and his daughter bounded into the den. "There you are. Hi, Daddy! G.G. and I had cocoa and Christmas cookies! Did you see the tree?"

"Hello, Sunshine." Feeling better and more hopeful than he had any right to, Ryan ruffled her hair. "Why don't you show it to me, and then we'll head home."

"But what about G.G.'s Christmas lights?"

"Your daddy can hang them another time," G.G. said.

A short while later, as Maggie shrugged into her parka, she glanced at him. "Can I write a letter to Santa tonight?"

"You bet. You can do that while I cook dinner."

As Maggie raced out the door, G.G. winked at Ryan. "Good luck."

"Thanks."

SITTING AT the kitchen table, pencil in hand, Maggie frowned in concentration at the sheet of wide-ruled paper before her. "How do you spell Tina?"

"T-i-n-a," Ryan said, as he shoved a meatloaf into the

oven. This was the perfect time for him and Maggie to talk. He sat down across from her. "What exactly are you asking Santa for?"

"It's a secret. How do you spell *mommy?*"

Ryan spelled the word, then eyed her. "Are you asking Santa to make Tina your mother?"

His daughter gaped at him. "How did you find out?"

As serious as the situation was, Ryan stifled a smile. "Just a lucky guess. Am I right?"

Maggie nodded, her eyes big and dark with worry. "Is it wrong to ask for that, Daddy?"

Reaching across the table he tweaked her nose. "If I were a kid, I'd want Tina for a mom, too. She's awfully busy, though. I don't know if she has time to be anybody's mother."

"I know that, Daddy." Maggie glanced at the table, then at him. "That's why I'm asking Santa. Maybe he'll help. You could ask him, too. We should marry Tina."

"We should, huh?"

Now that he'd admitted his feelings for Tina to himself, that sounded like a great idea. In no time at all, he'd moved from not wanting a relationship to seeing himself married again. Talk about nuts… He'd best take a step back and slow down. Heck, he didn't even know how she felt about him. Sure, she liked him and had enjoyed the sex they'd shared. But beyond that? He hadn't a clue; didn't know if she even wanted to get married.

"I don't know about that, but I sure miss her. She needs someone to take her to a party in Seattle Friday night, and I'm thinking about going over there. If that's okay with you."

"You mean you're gonna date her?"

"I'm thinking about it."

"But you always say you don't date."

"Maybe I changed my mind."

"You did?" She absorbed his words with growing excitement. "Goody! Maybe Santa *and* you can both talk to Tina. And then, if she wants to be my mommy, we can move to Seattle and everything."

The part about moving surprised Ryan. It meant Maggie had thought about this already, and that leaving the island was an option. He wasn't at all sure about that, and the anticipation he saw now in his daughter's eyes scared him. What if Tina turned them down? "Easy there, Sunshine. She might not want to go out with me, so don't get your hopes up."

"Okay, Daddy." She deflated like a popped balloon, but only for a moment. "Can I come with you to see her?"

"Not this time. G.G. invited you to spend the night at her house. She said something about making cookies and watching a movie in bed. What do you think?"

"I think, good."

Ryan hoped she didn't have any nightmares over there. He'd talk to G.G. about that.

"Would you mind if I called Tina right now, before dinner's ready?" he asked. "While I'm talking to her, you can finish your letter. I'll get you an envelope, too, and later I'll mail it for you."

"Okay. What about me? Do I get to talk to Tina?"

"When I'm through, I'll bring you the phone. Listen, don't tell her or anybody else about the mommy thing. For now, let's keep that a secret between you and me."

"And Santa?"

"And Santa." Ryan headed upstairs for his bedroom and some privacy, taking the stairs two at a time. Toed out of his shoes and settled against the headboard. Nervous as a kid about to call a girl for the first time, he dialed Tina's cell. She picked up on the second ring.

"Hello, Maggie," she said, sounding pleased.

"It's Ryan."

"Ryan," she said, switching to surprise. "Has something happened to Maggie?"

"She's fine."

"Oh. Then why…? Hello."

Not one to circle a subject, Ryan jumped in. "G.G. says you're having a company Christmas party Friday night and you don't have a date. I'd like to take you."

"G.G. *told* you that? I'm going to wring her neck."

He pictured her cheeks flushing, and he grinned. "Nothing to be embarrassed about. Well?"

"You don't have to take me, Ryan. I'm planning to go by myself, no problem."

"I want to. Is it a suit-and-tie thing—and what time should I pick you up?"

"You're asking me out?"

"Yeah."

But you don't date. He heard the words as clearly as if she'd spoken them. A chuckle bubbled from his chest. "What time does the party start, and how long does it take to get there from your place?"

"Um, seven. It's only a few miles from my apartment. And it's cocktail dress, so wear a suit and tie. Who's going to babysit Maggie?"

"G.G. offered."

"Naturally."

"So I'll be at your place at a quarter to seven."

Tina gave him directions. "What's this really about, Ryan?"

No way was he spilling his guts over the phone. "That

can wait until I see you. Now, Maggie wants to talk to you, so hang on."

Whistling, he carried the phone downstairs.

TINA FINISHED the final touches on her makeup and checked her appearance in the mirror. The fitted waist and flared skirt of her silver off-the-shoulder cocktail dress flattered her figure, and her shimmery hose and strappy black heels made her legs look longer.

"Not bad," she said to herself. She wondered what Ryan would think. He'd never seen her dressed up.

She couldn't quite believe that she actually had a date with him. Or that he was taking her to the company Christmas party. She hadn't brought anyone for years, and people were bound to wonder. Only June knew she was bringing someone. And of course, G.G. and Kate.

"What do you think it means?" she'd asked Kate on the phone the day before.

"That he wants something more with you, of course."

"But he made it perfectly clear that because Maggie comes first in his life, he doesn't want to get involved. Besides, it's been almost three weeks since I left the island. Why now?"

"Maybe he needed to think things through."

"But that doesn't make sense," she'd replied. "Especially since he lives on Halo Island and I'm in Seattle."

"So? We talked about this before. Lots of people have long-distance relationships."

"You're forgetting about Maggie."

"No, I'm not."

The conversation had ended with Tina promising to let Kate know what happened.

Soon enough Tina would find out.

At exactly six forty-five, the phone on the kitchen

wall rang. *Ryan.* Tina's insides fluttered, and she suddenly understood where the term "butterflies in your stomach" came from.

She picked up the phone. "Hi."

"I'm downstairs."

His deep voice caused every nerve in her body to hum with anticipation. "I'll buzz you in."

In no time he knocked on the door. Heart pounding, Tina opened it. He was wearing a black wool overcoat. Underneath, a black suit, crisp white shirt and red-and-green silk tie. As always, handsome and sexy enough to give a girl heart palpitations.

It had been nearly three weeks, and she strained toward him like a flower in need of light. "Hey, you," she said, sounding remarkably calm.

"Hello."

He kissed her, a brief, soft brush of his lips that left her aching for more. His warm, appreciative gaze combed over her, and she nearly melted at his feet.

"You look beautiful."

"Thanks. You look pretty good, yourself." Flushing and awash with love, she stood back to let him in. "I don't want to be late, so we should go. I'll grab my coat."

While she retrieved it from the closet, he glanced around her small living room, which she'd spent the previous night cleaning. "I like your place."

With Ryan's solid presence, somehow the room felt brighter and more alive. But then, so did Tina. "It's small, but comfortable enough for one person," she said.

During the drive to the party, he asked about her job. She wanted to tell him the truth—that she was unhappy and wished she could quit—but nobody in the world knew about that. Neither could she lie.

"I'm still learning," she said, which was the truth. "How are you?"

"Not bad." He updated her on Maggie, who was excited about Christmas and looking forward to seeing Tina.

While Tina was happy to hear about Ryan's daughter, she really wanted to talk about Ryan and his reasons for coming here. As they waited at a stoplight, she blurted out her question. "When are you going to tell me why you're here?"

The light turned green. "You know the answer to that— to take you to the Christmas party. And we're just about there." He signaled, then turned into the parking lot.

"But the other night, you said you wanted to talk."

"And I do." Ryan pulled into a slot and parked. In the streetlights, his eyes glittered. "But what I want to say— I don't want to be rushed. Now, if you'd rather head back to your place now and talk instead of going to this dinner party, that's fine with me. But I don't think your boss would like that."

He was right. Their talk would have to wait. Frustrated, Tina could only nod.

Ryan exited his side of the car and came around to help her out.

Was he planning to stay the night? Tina couldn't bring herself to ask. And she wasn't sure whether she'd let him stay or not. If she had any pride at all, she wouldn't. Yet, she'd changed the sheets on her bed.

Ryan opened her door and held out his hand, his grip warm and firm, and they ambled toward the low building. It was a cold, crisp night, and their breath hung in the air like smoke. Other people joined them, including Kendra and her date, who looked like a *GQ* model.

"Hello, there." Kendra shot Ryan a flirtatious look. "Who're you?"

"This is Kendra Eubanks," Tina said, wondering what Ryan would think of her. "Meet Ryan Chase."

"Delighted," she said, offering her hand. "This is my boyfriend, Todd Howe."

They exchanged hellos.

"So you're Kendra," Ryan said. He glanced at Tina and smiled.

"You've heard of me?" Kendra glanced at Tina. "What did you tell him?"

"It's all good," Ryan said, to Tina's relief.

"Have you two been dating long?" Kendra asked.

No telling why she wanted to know. Tina shook her head. "This is our first date."

"We met when Tina came to Halo Island to take care of G.G.," Ryan said. "My daughter and I live across the street."

"Ah." Kendra widened her eyes, then gave Tina a sly look. "No wonder you used your vacation to take care of her."

Tina rolled her eyes, but Ryan grinned.

"I never thought I'd say this," Kendra told him, "but Tina's turning out to be a great creative director."

Tina managed to hide her surprise. "Thank you. You're great to work with, too."

She felt Ryan stiffen. *Why?* But they'd reached the door and then she forgot about it. A uniformed guard checked off their names before allowing them into the lobby.

"What exactly is this place?" Ryan asked, taking in the creamy walls, art deco décor and huge Christmas tree made entirely of poinsettias.

"This is a private club Mr. Sperling belongs to. We hold our Christmas party here every year."

They checked their coats and headed for the well-appointed dining room. Tina couldn't help noticing the admiring glances of every woman in the room. And the speculative looks—but she'd expected those.

Over the next half hour she introduced Ryan to everyone in the company. Later, in the ladies' room, June grinned at her. "He's really something," she said.

"I know." Tina let out a heartfelt sigh.

"Oh, honey, you've got it bad." June had hugged her. "Well, from what I can see, so does he."

Tina didn't know about that, but she hoped June was right.

She and Ryan took their places at the round linen-covered table reserved for the senior employees and their partners—Jim and Marian Sperling, Tina and Ryan, and the company accountant and lawyers and their spouses. Completely at ease, Ryan conversed with these high-powered people as if he'd known them for years. Tina was impressed, and more in love than ever. And so curious about what would happen later that she hardly could stand it.

By the end of the evening, her ulcer hadn't so much as twinged. With Ryan beside her, everything seemed *more*. She'd eaten heartily, laughed hard at the comedian who'd been hired as entertainment and thoroughly enjoyed herself.

Several times she caught Ryan looking at her, his eyes dark with emotion. June was right, he *did* have feelings for her. The knowledge made her dizzy with happiness.

As she exchanged good-nights with everyone, Ryan's arm stayed around her waist. Desire and love flooded her, and she was eager to go home, talk and fall into his arms.

Chapter Seventeen

"Nice party," Ryan said as he drove back to Tina's place.

"It always is. Thanks for coming with me."

"No problem." In the light from the street and the oncoming cars, he noted her warm expression. "Your boss is a class act, and the rest of the employees seem nice. With people like that in the company, I see why you love your job. "

Watching her interact with her colleagues had been interesting. And very enlightening. Everyone liked and admired her, and she seemed to like them.

"It is a good place to work, and as creative director I'm next in line to be CEO." She turned away, to look out her window. "Everyone assumes that someday I'll take over Jim Sperling's job."

Though her face was hidden from Ryan, he detected not a shred of discontent. He certainly had seen nothing but laughter and good feelings tonight. Tina seemed pleased with her life, and as ambitious as ever. *Man, G.G., did you ever get it wrong.*

Earlier, he'd been certain Tina cared about him and wanted more. Now, he wasn't so sure. *She belongs here, in this world.*

Not on Halo Island. A heavy feeling settled in his gut and chest—made worse because at the moment she wouldn't even look at him. Call him a coward, but if she rejected him he simply couldn't handle it. Not tonight. Hell, not ever.

What in the world had made him think Tina wanted more than a job?

Feeling like a sorry fool, he found a parking place near her apartment building. He thought about dropping her off, driving to Anacortes and catching the ferry home, but the last one had left hours ago. Besides, she was expecting that talk—the talk he no longer wanted to have.

They rode the elevator in silence, Ryan mulling over what he could say that didn't involve sharing his feelings and making a fool of himself.

Inside, Tina took his coat and hung it up. While he stood nearby, with his hands in his trouser pockets and dread in his belly.

"Would you like a glass of wine?" she asked.

"I've had enough, thanks."

She sat at one end of the sofa, leaving plenty of room for him. As miserable as Ryan felt, he couldn't sit next to her. He took a chair instead, holding on to the arms with fingers that were stiff.

She tilted her head, and tiny lines appeared between her eyebrows. "You wanted to talk?"

Maggie and the bank were safe topics. "Dr. Wright— that therapist I took Maggie to—said the same things you did. That if I'm not happy, Maggie won't be." She gave a knowing nod, and Ryan plunged into a new topic. "I don't know if you heard that Halo Island Bank will be sold off next year?"

"I hadn't."

"It was just announced this week. Dr. Wright thinks I should buy it. Thing is, if I do, I won't have much time for Maggie. But you and I already talked about that." He scratched the back of his neck. "I still don't know what to do."

In the silence that hung between them, Tina's face went from curious to irritated. Ryan started to loosen his tie, then thought better of it.

"This is what you wanted to discuss? You could have saved yourself the trip and called. I'm not stupid, Ryan. I know that you're only here because G.G. asked you to come. I can't believe I thought... Never mind." She gave him a hurt look that made him feel about two inches tall.

"Yes, this was G.G.'s idea, but I'm here because I wanted to see you," Ryan said, forgetting to steer clear of his feelings.

"Right. That's why you waited almost three weeks to do it." She rolled her eyes at the ceiling. "Look, if you want to buy the bank but you're concerned about Maggie, just ask her what she thinks about it. Problem solved."

He'd never considered that. "That's a great idea. I will."

Her lips tightened and formed a thin line. She was still upset with him, which was his cue to cut and run.

He cleared his throat. "It's late. I should go." And find a room someplace. He stood.

"I just want to get one thing straight." Tina sat back and regarded him through slightly narrowed eyes. "This whole evening, those tender looks and your arm around me... What was that about? Do you care about me or not?"

"Sure I do." He shifted his weight. "But you've got your high-powered job to worry about, and I don't want Maggie getting hurt."

"You should know by now that I love Maggie. I lo— I care about you, too, unfortunately way more than I should. Lots of people juggle jobs and families." Tina picked up a throw pillow and hugged it. "You know darned well I'm not like those other women who walked out on you, so what is your problem?" Before he could get in a word, her eyes widened. "You're afraid. Not only for Maggie, but for yourself."

Bull's-eye. Ryan hated that she'd figured him out, and he hated the disappointment in her face. *Take a chance and tell her how you feel, lunkhead.*

He swallowed. "You're right, I'm scared spitless." He sat back down, this time beside her. "The truth is, I came here to talk about a lot more than whether I should buy the bank. And I will, but first there's something you should read." He reached into his jacket pocket and pulled out the envelope containing Maggie's letter. "Maggie wrote this to Santa," he said, handing it to Tina.

He watched her face as she read the misspelled, laboriously penciled letter. Which was only one sentence. *Der Santa, plez let Tina bee my momy.*

"Oh, Ryan." Tina bit her lip. Her eyes filled. "I don't know what to say."

"Since I'm the one who's supposed to be talking, that's okay."

With his thumb, he brushed away her tears. She was so beautiful, and he was so overcome with tenderness that for a moment words failed him. For the second time he cleared his throat. "Living without you the past few weeks… I've missed you. I can be thickheaded, and it took me a while to figure out that I love you. That's what I came here to say. And why I couldn't take my eyes off you all night, and why I needed to touch you."

He wanted to touch her now, but didn't. This next part was hard, and he glanced down. "Seeing you with your work friends and listening to them sing your praises… It's pretty obvious how important your job is to you. I figured you'd reject me. I didn't want to hear that, so I kept my mouth shut."

"Wait a minute." She touched his cheek. "Did you say you loved me?"

"Guilty as charged."

Shaking her head, tears streaming down her face, she looked at him. This time when his collar felt too tight, he loosened it. "For God's sake, say something."

"Oh, Ryan. If you only knew…. I love you, too."

"Then quit bawling and kiss me."

Her lips were soft and warm, *home*. Ryan realized it didn't matter where he and Maggie lived, as long as Tina was there. *He might as well go for broke.* "I know this is kind of sudden, but the past few days I've been thinking a lot about us. If you want, Maggie and I could move to Seattle, to be with you. You'd have to move to a bigger place, though."

"You'd do that for me? But you love Halo Island."

That was true, but his happiness was at stake. "I love you more."

He kissed her again, this time with more heat and passion. Tina pulled back, flushed and nervous. "You and Maggie living here—that won't work."

"Okay, we'll start slower, and give this thing between us more time to grow."

"That's not what I mean, Ryan." She swallowed and smoothed down the skirt of her dress. "There's something you should know. Something I've never shared."

Uh-oh. Warily, he waited.

"The truth is, I don't like my job. In fact, I'm close to hating it. I don't sleep well, and I'm no fun to be around. I couldn't ask you and Maggie to live with that."

Ryan couldn't believe what he was hearing. "Say what?"

"I've tried and tried to love my work, but it's no use." With a heavy sigh, she knotted her hands in her lap. "I used to live and breathe advertising, but gradually over the past few years, that's changed. I've lost my passion for it."

Thoroughly confused, he frowned. "Could've fooled me."

"You, G.G., Jefferson and everyone else. I'm good at pretending, but I've paid for it with an ulcer, insomnia and an empty life."

"I don't get it," he said. "Why?"

"You know what G.G. and everyone else wants—for me to someday run CE Marketing." She started to nibble at her lip. "They don't just *want* it, they *expect* it of me, and they have for some time. I can't just up and change my mind. They'd never understand."

Ryan sure didn't. "It's the twenty-first century. People change jobs all the time," he said. "I certainly have, and it's no big deal."

"It's a huge deal for me. G.G. and Jefferson and the rest of the neighbors have been so good to me. They helped raise me, and they put me through undergraduate and graduate school. Not one of them will let me pay back a penny of that money. They all say they'll get their return when I run the company."

Never had Ryan imagined anything like this. Dumbfounded, he scratched the back of his neck. "That's crazy. They love you. I'll bet if you explain…"

"Don't you get it?" She sounded both frustrated and

agonized. "I. Can't. Let. Them. Down. And what about Jim Sperling? He just hired me. If I left now…" She gave her head a dismal shake.

"Tina. Listen to me." Ryan cupped her face and drew her close. "The advice you and Dr. Wright gave me—that if I was happy, Maggie would be, too? That also applies to you and the people who care about you. If you're happy, they'll be happy. As for Jim Sperling, trust me, he'll get over it."

She looked skeptical, so he went at it from a different angle. "Tell me, if you didn't have to worry about anybody else, what would you do?"

"Quit CE Marketing and consult, part-time, from the island."

"You'd move to Halo Island?"

"In a New York second."

This was the best news yet. Ryan grinned. "Then, do it."

She rolled her eyes. "Did you not hear what I said? I can't do that."

"Once you level with G.G., Jefferson and the rest of them, you can. When you do, I'll be standing beside you."

He saw that he hadn't convinced her. And suddenly he understood the *real* reason for her constraint. Fear. "You're scared they'll stop loving you," he said.

"No, I'm not. I…" She hesitated, then gazed at him in wonder. "You're right. I never realized. How did you know?"

"It makes sense. You don't have a thing to worry about, Tina. People don't love you for what you do, but for who you are. You could turn into a bag lady and they'd still love you. I would."

"Really?"

He nodded. "And so would they."

"You're probably right. Maybe." Indecision clouded her face. "I so want to believe you, but can I think about it?"

"Sure." Ryan put his arm around her shoulders, and she settled against him. "What do you think about kids?" he asked.

"I love them, of course. Especially Maggie."

"I know how you feel about her. Do you want to have any of your own?"

"Someday, I'd like a whole houseful."

"I like kids, too." Time to pop the question. Pivoting to face her, Ryan clasped her hands in his. "And I'd like to make them with you. Whatever you decide to do career-wise and wherever you want to live is okay by me—as long as we're together. Is it too soon in our relationship to propose? Because I know I want to marry you, and nothing will change that."

"Oh, Ryan." She beamed at him. "Yes. That is, no, it's not too soon. I've dreamed about this since I first met you and Maggie."

He'd never felt so happy. "I love you, Tina."

After several long, intense kisses, he broke away. "I want to show you how much I love you, but not on the sofa." He stood, pulling her up with him. "Where's the bedroom?"

An hour later, Tina snuggled against Ryan's side. He held her close and kissed the top of her head. He loved her and would stand by her no matter what, and she'd never felt so content or happy.

Even if everyone else abandoned her for letting them down. *Stop thinking like that, silly.*

Her rational mind understood that they would love her no matter what, but her heart wasn't convinced. Possibly because she'd lost her mother and father so young, and feared she'd lose her acquired family, too. A thought that terrified her. Yep, that was the reason.

"Suddenly, you're all tensed up," Ryan said. "I'll bet I know why."

He sat up and flipped on the bedside lamp. Tina squinted in the sudden light.

"Sit up, babe," he said.

Tina did.

He gently tilted her chin so that she looked into his eyes. His warm, loving eyes.

"Repeat after me," he said. "No matter what I do in life, I'm lovable. The people who love me now will always love me."

"Do I have to?"

"Uh-huh."

"Slave driver." Feeling somewhat ridiculous, Tina obeyed. "No matter what I do in life, I'm lovable. The people who love me now will always love me."

Ryan kissed the tip of her nose. "Good. Now prove it."

It was time to trust them. "All right, I'll tell them today or tomorrow." Before she lost her nerve. She swallowed. "But if you're wrong…"

"Then we'll deal with it. How do you want to do it?"

"Get it over with and tell them all at the same time." Counting Jefferson Jeffries and everyone on the cul-de-sac except the Featherstones, who'd moved in long after Tina had finished school, there were a good number of people involved.

"Then I'll throw a neighborhood party at my place tonight."

"On the spur of the moment, with Christmas in two weeks? I'm sure people have plans."

"Maybe, but by now they all know I spent the night with you. And when you come back with me today, when no one expects you for another week…?" Ryan smiled. "Believe me, they'll make time to stop by. Now, it's late, and I want to leave for the island first thing in the morning, so how about I turn off the light and we get some sleep?"

He extinguished the lamp, and once again Tina settled into his side—the second night of a lifetime of sleeping beside the man she loved. Oh, that was a lovely feeling.

She closed her eyes. Yet as tired as she was, thoughts continued to whirl through her head. Now that she'd made up her mind to tell G.G. and the others the truth, she felt better. Still scared, but tons lighter. Which was strange, since she'd never realized how her secret had weighed her down. As soon as she told the people she loved, she'd let Mr. Sperling know. And recommend Kendra to take her place. Wouldn't she be surprised?

That'd take care of *her* loose ends. But what about Ryan's?

"Ryan?"

"Hmm?"

"Are you asleep?"

"Not anymore." He snuggled her closer and nuzzled her neck. "What's up? Besides a certain part of my body."

Her undeniable physical need almost obliterated her other thoughts. But before she lost herself in loving him, she needed to know. "Are you going to buy the bank?"

"That depends on what Maggie thinks."

"I hope she likes the idea." Tina hooked her thigh over Ryan's hip, so that his arousal was flush with the part of her that most craved physical contact. "Do you think she'll be happy about us?"

Ryan groaned. "I know she will. This is what she asked Santa for. But I don't want to talk about Maggie right now."

He kissed her, then lifted her to straddle him.

Eager and hungry, Tina let out a needy sound as she eased herself onto his shaft. "Something tells me we won't be sleeping much tonight."

Ryan gripped her hips. "Something tells me you're right."

SATURDAY NIGHT, the neighbors, Jefferson Jeffries and Kate and her family crowded into Ryan's house. Aside from Kate and family, this gathering was not so different from the November potluck. But Tina felt as if she'd grown by worlds. So much had changed in such a short time.

In a little while she'd share her feelings, and she'd never been so anxious, not even when she'd lost her father and didn't know what would happen to her.

Avoiding G.G.'s and Kate's questions hadn't been easy, either. Since this morning, when she'd called to let them know about tonight, they'd pushed and prodded for information. Tina had put them off. Even so, Kate guessed about the engagement, and G.G. had hinted that she knew, too.

But neither had a clue about the rest of it.

"You didn't eat your gingerbread boy," Maggie said. She was overjoyed to see Tina, and had shadowed her constantly while she helped Ryan ready his house for tonight. "Don't you like it?"

What to say? That at the moment she couldn't eat, not even if her life depended on it? She forced a smile. "I love it, sweetie. But I'm saving it for later. There's Sam. Why don't you see if she wants one?"

Maggie scampered off.

From across the room, Ryan was involved in an earnest discussion with Jack Burrows, Kate's husband, and Harry Featherstone. He glanced up and caught Tina staring at him. His face softened and lit up with love, and her fears abated.

He arched his eyebrows. *Are you ready?*

Suddenly, she was. She nodded. Ryan excused himself and joined her.

He caught her cold hand in his warm grip, and they made their way to the Christmas tree in the corner, stopping to bring Maggie along.

The room quieted in a rush of expectation and excitement, with furtive smiles everywhere.

"Tina and I have an announcement to make," Ryan said.

They waited while everyone crowded closer, G.G. and Kate already beaming.

Ryan winked at Maggie. "You're getting an early Christmas present, Sunshine."

"I am?" Maggie clapped and jumped up and down. Standing with Kate, Sam did the same.

Tina took the little girl's hand. "That's right. Your daddy and I are getting married. I'm going to be your mommy."

Whistles, applause and cheers broke out. Over the noise, Maggie squealed. "Yippee!" Then her face crumpled and she started to cry.

"Sweetie." Tina crouched down in front of her. "What's the matter?"

"I'm so happy," Maggie wailed.

Everyone laughed. Tina hugged her close. "I love you," she said. "And from now on, if you want, you can call me Mommy."

"There's more," Ryan said.

Maggie sniffled and pulled away, and Tina straightened.

It was time. Holding Ryan's hand, her throat tight with emotion, she spoke from the heart. "Ryan, Maggie and I are going to live here, in this house." She paused, looking G.G. and everyone else in the eye. "I'm sorry to let you all down, but I plan to give my notice Monday morning."

"Let us down? Are you kidding?" G.G. dismissed her announcement with an airy wave. "You've found the man of your dreams and he's found you. We don't care about that job."

"That's right," Rose said. "Jobs come and go, but when love comes your way, you'd better grab it." She smiled at Sidney, who turned beet-red.

Then he nodded, and so did Jefferson and everyone else in the room.

Stunned, Tina gaped at the entire group. "But, I thought... You keep saying that you expect me to run the company someday, and that when I do, your investment in my education will pay off."

G.G. sniffed. "We only wanted that because you did. What we care about is that you're happy."

"Really?" Overcome with feeling, Tina covered her mouth with her hand. "I can't believe I was so afraid to tell you." Tears welled in her eyes.

"This is no time for tears," Sidney said. "Buck up, girl."

"Hush, Sidney." Rose elbowed him.

He glared at her, then broke into a wide smile. "Congratulations, both of you. I hope that someday you're able to bicker and enjoy each other's company as much as Rose and I do."

Rose tittered like a teenage girl.

"If this hadn't happened, I'd be in trouble," Kate said, winking. "Now I won't have to eat my apron. This is the best news I've heard in months."

For the first time in ages, Tina felt lighthearted and

carefree. "You were right, Ryan," she said. "Thank you for pushing me to talk to them."

"I'm happy for you." He squeezed her hand.

Ready to relax and enjoy herself, Tina started toward Kate.

"However…" Jefferson said in a stern voice.

Tina froze.

"It's all over town that you gave notice on Monday, Ryan."

"Yes, and now I wish I'd listened to you and left my money in that other bank." Rose gave her head a sorrowful shake. "Without you, Halo Island Bank will be a dismal place, indeed."

"Raising a child is expensive," Sidney said. "Without that job…"

"That's what I'm saying." Jefferson nodded. "I want to know what you two jobless people intend to do with yourselves."

"*Now* do you see now why I was so nervous about this?" Tina muttered to Ryan.

"Ryan has plenty of money," G.G. said, without a trace of concern. "He and Tina will be fine."

"Money or not, they're way too young to laze around all day," Jefferson said.

"Excuse me," Tina said. "We're right here. And we know that."

"I'm glad for your concerns, everyone, and if you wait one second, I may have an answer for you." Ryan hunkered down to Maggie's level. "Halo Island Bank is for sale," he said. "I want to buy it and turn it into a *successful* bank. Thing is, if I do, I'll be bringing work home at night, and I might work part of every weekend. How do you feel about that?"

"That's okay, Daddy, 'cause while you work I can play with Sam and Gina and my other friends."

"Awesome!" Sam pumped her fist into the air, causing smiles everywhere.

"You're positive?" Ryan said.

Maggie nodded. "When I'm tired of playing with my friends, I can be with my mommy, right?"

Mommy. A name that signified warmth, joy, love and security. Feeling like the luckiest woman in the world, Tina smiled at the child she loved as her own. "Absolutely."

"Tina?" Ryan asked, standing. "Are you sure about this?"

"If this is what you want, go for it," she said, taking his hand.

"Then I'll be putting in an offer to buy the Halo Island Bank."

"Hallelujah," Rose said.

Sidney whistled, and everyone else called out good wishes.

Still holding Tina's hand, Ryan turned to her. "If the bank deal goes through, and I own the bank, will you handle the advertising and promotion?"

She didn't have to think long about that. "I'd love to. I guess that means neither one of us will be unemployed, after all."

Everyone crowded around for hugs and congratulations. And more questions.

"Exactly when are you two getting married?" Norma Featherstone asked, cupping her pregnant belly. "Because I'm due in four months and I don't want to miss the wedding."

"Way before you deliver, right, babe?" Ryan asked.

Eager to marry him, Tina nodded. "The sooner, the better."

"Jack and I would like to make your cake," Kate offered. "Just tell us when and where, and what kind you want."

"There's not enough time to plan a Christmas wedding," G.G. said. "But if we start now, we could we could pull something together by New Year's Eve. We'll have it at my house."

"Perfect," Ryan and Tina said in unison.

And it was.

* * * * *

Look for Ann Roth's next story
set on Halo Island,
THE PILOT'S WOMAN
Coming in March 2008 only from
Harlequin American Romance.

Brad shoved the truck into gear and drove to the bottom of the hill, where the road forked. Turn left, and he'd be home in five minutes. Turn right, and he was headed for Indian Rock.

He had no damn business going to Indian Rock.

He had nothing to say to Meg McKettrick, and if he never set eyes on the woman again, it would be two weeks too soon.

He turned right.

He couldn't have said why.

He just drove straight to the Dixie Dog Drive-In.

Back in the day, he and Meg used to meet at the Dixie Dog, by tacit agreement, when either of them had been away. It had been some kind of universe thing, purely intuitive.

Passing familiar landmarks, Brad told himself he ought to turn around. The old days were gone. Things had ended badly between him and Meg anyhow, and she wasn't going to be at the Dixie Dog.

He kept driving.

He rounded a bend, and there was the Dixie Dog. Its big neon sign, a giant hot dog, was all lit up and going through its corny sequence—first it was covered in red squiggles of light, meant to suggest ketchup, and then yellow, for mustard.

Brad pulled into one of the slots next to a speaker, rolled down the truck window and ordered.

A girl roller-skated out with the order about five minutes later.

When she wheeled up to the driver's window, smiling, her eyes went wide with recognition, and she dropped the tray with a clatter.

Silently Brad swore. Damn if he hadn't forgotten he was a famous country singer.

The girl, a skinny thing wearing too much eye makeup, immediately started to cry. "I'm sorry!" she sobbed, squatting to gather up the mess.

"It's okay," Brad answered quietly, leaning to look down at her, catching a glimpse of her plastic name tag. "It's okay, Mandy. No harm done."

"I'll get you another dog and a shake right away, Mr. O'Ballivan!"

"Mandy?"

She stared up at him pitifully, sniffling. Thanks to the copious tears, most of the goop on her eyes had slid south. "Yes?"

"When you go back inside, could you not mention seeing me?"

"But you're Brad O'Ballivan!"

"Yeah," he answered, suppressing a sigh. "I know."

She rolled a little closer. "You wouldn't happen to have a picture you could autograph for me, would you?"

"Not with me," Brad answered.

"You could sign this napkin, though," Mandy said. "It's only got a little chocolate on the corner."

Brad took the paper napkin and her order pen, and

scrawled his name. Handed both items back through the window.

She turned and whizzed back toward the side entrance to the Dixie Dog.

Brad waited, marveling that he hadn't considered incidents like this one before he'd decided to come back home. In retrospect, it seemed shortsighted, to say the least, but the truth was, he'd expected to be—Brad O'Ballivan.

Presently Mandy skated back out again, and this time she managed to hold on to the tray.

"I didn't tell a soul!" she whispered. "But Heather and Darlene *both* asked me why my mascara was all smeared." Efficiently she hooked the tray onto the bottom edge of the window.

Brad extended payment, but Mandy shook her head.

"The boss said it's on the house, since I dumped your first order on the ground."

He smiled. "Okay, then. Thanks."

Mandy retreated, and Brad was just reaching for the food when a bright red Blazer whipped into the space beside his. The driver's door sprang open, crashing into the metal speaker, and somebody got out in a hurry.

Something quickened inside Brad.

And in the next moment Meg McKettrick was standing practically on his running board, her blue eyes blazing.

Brad grinned. "I guess you're not over me after all," he said.

SPECIAL EDITION™

brings you a heartwarming
new McKettrick's story from

NEW YORK TIMES BESTSELLING AUTHOR

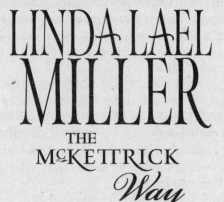

LINDA LAEL MILLER

THE McKETTRICK *Way*

Meg McKettrick is surprised to be reunited
with her high school flame, Brad O'Ballivan,
who has returned home to his family's
neighboring ranch. After seeing Meg again,
Brad realizes he still loves her. But the pride
of both manage to interfere with love...until
an unexpected matchmaker gets involved.

—— McKettrick Women ——

Available December wherever you buy books.

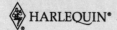

Kate Merrill had grown up convinced
that the most attractive men were incapable
of ever settling down. Yet the harder she
resisted the superstar photographer
Tyler Nichols, the more persistent the
handsome world traveler became.
So by the time Christmas arrived, there
was only one wish on her holiday list—
that she was wrong!

LOOK FOR

THE CHRISTMAS DATE

BY

Michele Dunaway

Available December
wherever you buy books

REQUEST YOUR FREE BOOKS!
2 FREE NOVELS PLUS 2
FREE GIFTS!

American **ROMANCE**®

Heart, Home & Happiness!

YES! Please send me 2 FREE Harlequin American Romance® novels and my 2 FREE gifts. After receiving them, if I don't wish to receive any more books, I can return the shipping statement marked "cancel." If I don't cancel, I will receive 4 brand-new novels every month and be billed just $4.24 per book in the U.S., or $4.99 per book in Canada, plus 25¢ shipping and handling per book and applicable taxes, if any*. That's a savings of close to 15% off the cover price! I understand that accepting the 2 free books and gifts places me under no obligation to buy anything. I can always return a shipment and cancel at any time. Even if I never buy another book from Harlequin, the two free books and gifts are mine to keep forever.

154 HDN EEZK   354 HDN EEZV

Name	(PLEASE PRINT)	

Address		Apt. #

City	State/Prov.	Zip/Postal Code

Signature (if under 18, a parent or guardian must sign)

Mail to the **Harlequin Reader Service**®:
IN U.S.A.: P.O. Box 1867, Buffalo, NY 14240-1867
IN CANADA: P.O. Box 609, Fort Erie, Ontario L2A 5X3

Not valid to current Harlequin American Romance subscribers.

Want to try two free books from another line?
Call 1-800-873-8635 or visit www.morefreebooks.com.

* Terms and prices subject to change without notice. NY residents add applicable sales tax. Canadian residents will be charged applicable provincial taxes and GST. This offer is limited to one order per household. All orders subject to approval. Credit or debit balances in a customer's account(s) may be offset by any other outstanding balance owed by or to the customer. Please allow 4 to 6 weeks for delivery.

Your Privacy: Harlequin is committed to protecting your privacy. Our Privacy Policy is available online at www.eHarlequin.com or upon request from the Reader Service. From time to time we make our lists of customers available to reputable firms who may have a product or service of interest to you. If you would prefer we not share your name and address, please check here.

NEW YORK TIMES
BESTSELLING AUTHOR

DIANA PALMER

has done it again—created
a Long Tall Texans
readers will fall in love with...

IRON COWBOY

*Available March 2008
wherever you buy books.*

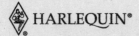

HARLEQUIN®

American ROMANCE®

COMING NEXT MONTH

#1189 THE RANCHER'S CHRISTMAS BABY by Cathy Gillen Thacker
Texas Legacies: The Carrigans

As teenagers, best friends Amy Carrigan and Teddy McCabe promised each other that if they didn't find their soul mates by thirty, they'd start their own family. Now, with Amy's biological clock ticking overtime, the sexy rancher decides to pop the question. But marriage brings more than they bargained for. Will love bloom in time to ring in the New Year with a Carrigan/McCabe baby?

#1190 TEXAN FOR THE HOLIDAYS by Victoria Chancellor
Brody's Crossing

No sooner has Scarlett shouted, "California, here I come!" than her clunker of a car breaks down. But there are worse places to be stranded than Brody's Crossing, especially when local lawyer James Brody is dying to show her how they celebrate the holidays in their quaint Texas town. Scarlett promised herself she'd be in Los Angeles by the New Year…but she's feeling more Texan by the minute!

#1191 THE CHRISTMAS DATE by Michele Dunaway

Kate Merrill had grown up convinced that the most attractive men were incapable of ever settling down. Yet the harder she resisted superstar photographer Tyler Nichols, the more persistent the handsome world traveler became. So by the time Christmas arrived, there was only one wish on her holiday list—that she was wrong!

#1192 WITH THIS RING by Lee McKenzie
A Convenient Proposal

Brent Borden had always imagined that Leslie Durrance was happy on her pedestal. Until she ran—in a thunderstorm, dripping diamonds, wedding dress and all—into the construction worker's arms. This was Brent's chance to show the poor little rich girl that maybe Mr. *Right* could come from the *wrong* side of town.

www.eHarlequin.com

HARCNM1107